GW00568946

The Voyage of Mael Duin

IRELAND

The Voyage of Mael Duin

Patricia Aakhus McDowell

WOLFHOUND PRESS

First published 1991 by
WOLFHOUND PRESS
68 Mountjoy Square
Dublin 1

First published in Ireland, UK and Europe by
Wolfhound Press 1991

First edition: Santa Cruz 1989

Wolfhound Press receives financial assistance from The Arts Council (An Chomhairle Ealaíon), Dublin, Ireland.

British Library Cataloguing in Publication Data

McDowell, Patricia Aakhus
   The voyage of Mael Duin.
   I. Title
   813.54   [F]

ISBN 0-86327-309-2

Cover design: Jan de Fouw
Illustrated by Michael Aakhus
Printed by Billings & Sons, Worcester

THE VOYAGE
OF MAEL DUIN

FOR BETSY MCDOWELL
AND GRACE NICHOLS

Introduction

In the vaults of Trinity College Library, there is a medieval manuscript called *The Yellow Book of Lecan*. In dark sepia, hand-lettered Old Irish, the story of *The Voyage of Mael Duin's Curragh* begins:

"Do Eoganacht Ninais Do Mael Duin ar mbunudus. Ailill acher agha a athair trenfer essede daglaech tigerna a cheneoil fen. Maccailleach banaircinneach cille cailleach a mathair."

"Mael Duin was of the tribe of the Eoganacht of Ninuss. Ailill Ochair Agha was his father—a big man, a fierce warrior and chieftain of his own tuath. His mother was a young nun. It is in this way that his conception came to pass."

The story continues. He is given to a queen who raises him as her own child, a chieftain's heir. When he is sixteen he accidentally discovers his true parentage, and in seeking his own kin finds his mother insane and his father—unavenged—killed by raiders.

Until he has avenged his father's death he is an outcast. His official status is lower than that of a murderer or a lunatic. A druid helps him build a huge curragh, choose a crew, and divine the most fortuitous day for departure. With sixteen young men, including his friend Diuran Leccerd, the "half-poet," who is studying the draoidheacht (the druid worship), Mael Duin sets off on the western sea in pursuit of the raiders.

He finds their island quickly, but a storm comes up. Lost in strange seas, Mael Duin's curragh rides winds and currents from one nightmare island to the next.

The Celtic Revival produced several edited versions of this epic. In the Victorian *Old Celtic Romances*, Patrick Joyce included an expurgated "translation" in which Mael Duin's natural mother is a queen rather than a nun.

In all versions the islands unfold randomly, and even in its purest form—in the manuscript called *The Yellow Book of Lecan*, the medieval scribes gave the voyage a heavy Christian slant, disguising and underplaying pagan elements. And all—including the scribes—were working with fragments.

Scholars Joyce and Oskamp (author of a recent literal translation) have considered the *Voyage a* contrived assimilation of other literary voyages, rather than an ancient, original and significant work of oral tradition.

However, when one examines the islands singly, looking for clues in folklore, geography and archeology, one begins to feel differently. By rearranging them, the backbone of the epic appears, like a skeleton emerging slowly out of the sand. When one takes a hard look at the two-dimensional Mael Duin with respect to his circumstances, he begins to put on flesh and blood.

It is generally held that pagan Ireland assimilated early Christianity easily and without relinquishing much belief in and practice of magic. One of the early Irish bishops reputedly said, "Christ is my druid." The *Voyage* is set in that time of blurred differences, but it seems likely that the monks who later wrote it down made some "improvements," embellishing the story with Christian morals and motives. According to the manuscript, when the storm blows Mael Duin off course, he decides to drift "wherever God wills it." Such passivity, while appropriate to an ascetic of the early church, makes little sense in the context of an heroic epic. It robs the story of dramatic tension, and deprives the *resolution* of the narrative—one which is unique in epic literature—of impact. The story ends before it has begun; the rest is a cataloguing of islands. But if one removes the deadly device, the story has life again; Mael Duin is in pursuit.

This quest belongs to the oldest genre. Despite the

imperfections of the text, it is, as Frank O'Connor put it in *A Short History of Irish Literature—A Backward Glance*, a piece of primary literature:

". . . When an oral tradition comes into contact with a written tradition—preferably one that is not too highly developed—it may produce literature of the highest quality, autonomous and primary in the way of Greek and Hebrew literature.

"I mean that it is in the main original, not derivative, and expresses the joys and fears of man confronted with an unfamiliar universe. The shock of man's fundamental experience set down as though for the first time.

"What the early Irish really thought of the stars is something we may never know; the early missionaries did too good a job of destruction. I know of only two stories that give any impression of the gravity of primitive religious thought. One is *The Wooing of Etain*, the other is *The Voyage of Mael Duin*."

The surrealistic islands have a strange, vivid reality that records the "shock of man's fundamental experience." The odd, speechless birds of the second island actually do live on Little Skellig off the Iveragh Peninsula (and that's the only place in the world they live). The fountains, columns of crystal and giant forges boiling the sea are, in fact, geysers, icebergs and volcanoes near Iceland.

But it is the richness of Irish magic that pervades the voyage—the virtues of salmon; rowan-berries and apples as the fruit of the triple goddess; the belief that hell, with its rivers of fire, is in the north; sacred wells, birds with human souls, the impassable bridge of glass; the nightmares of giant insects, of domestic animals turning on man; the cults of smiths and millers. Half-forgotten rituals come alive: sacrifices, the echtress (horse feast), fasting against an enemy. Taboos masked as challenges must be passed. Failure to act correctly results in horror,

9

insanity, or death.

However interesting as psychological or cultural ar-
chetypes, the islands, in their random order, are unsatis-
fying in terms of story. But when rearranged as a Irish
Book of the Dead, energized by Mael Duin's desire, they
begin to make sense; they are, as the poet Robert Graves
wrote, "capable of raising the hair on the back of the
neck."

The islands in the West teach Mael Duin how to die
and how to live. In his quest for revenge he must change
from a man of brutality and unteachable ignorance to a
man of compassion. He must learn providence and
magic. And proportion is everything: The Irish relativity
of time/place/matter and common transformations may
appear dreamlike, but they are as logical as nature.

The Island of Women (which receives no particular
stress in the manuscript or other versions), as the home
of the goddess, determines finally what Mael Duin must
become. The epic turns around the incest/patricide myth
of the triple goddess—the story of the son who displaces
the father as consort to the queen, assuring with his rise
that the world will renew itself, harvest and spring return. At the crisis in which Mael Duin comes close to
suicide he glimpses the truth: It isn't his father but his
mother he must confront—the goddess in her third face,
the Hag—death, madness and vulnerability, which he
has never acknowledged.

I have invented a narrative frame around the voyage,
in which Diuran Leccerd, half-poet, or half-druid, and
Mael Duin's companion on the voyage, tells the story to
the monk Mael Muire. It was a Mael Muire, abbot of the
monastery of Clonmacnoise, who copied fragments of
the voyage—virtually identical to those found in *The
Yellow Book of Lecan*—in the manuscript, *The Book of the
Dun Cow.*

PROLOGUE

1

I

Is acher in gaith in-noct
Ju-fuasna fairggae findfolt;
Ni agor reimm mora minn
Dond laechraid lainn ua Lothlind.

The wind is rough tonight,
It blows the ocean's white hair
I do not fear the fierce Vikings
Crossing the Irish sea.

Written in the margin of a 9th-century Irish manuscript

One evening in early spring of the year 839, the wind blew hard off the River Shannon. Through the long twilight and into the dark the wind blew. At the monastery of Clonmacnoise, in the great meadow one hundred miles from the sea, the river broke into the grass below the watchtower, and over the steps that led to the courtyard and the cathedral. In the fields beyond the chapels and the sleeping quarters, the forge and the stables, cattle and sheep slept under a stone wall out of the hard wind, and the boy with his black and white dog slept too. When a lamb cried the dog lifted her head, and went back to sleep.

The watchtower at Clonmacnoise, the *cloigtheach*, had an entrance above the ground, with a rope ladder that the monks could pull up after them. There was an alarm bell, and a window more than a hundred feet above the river, to watch for ships. But that evening, because of the wind, the cloigtheach was empty. In the grass below the

12

tower the river left branches, with masses of leaves, and stripped of leaves, a bird's nest woven with lamb fleece— the wool still white, but soaked and pierced by sharp twigs.

At one o'clock the wind changed and the clouds began to break up. Stars came out, and a full moon shone on the river. In the courtyard, the old sundial became a moondial, with a chink of black falling back from the gnomon. It was there, on that same day, on his way to mass, that Abbot Mael Muire had found his son Eoin. It was Mael Muire's fiftieth birthday. Eoin had ridden two days straight from St. Kevin's monastery on the east coast, where he was priest, to surprise him. He stood by the sundial, waiting, braced against the wind. Eoin was twenty-eight, with his mother's direct blue eyes and quick, shy smile, but dark-haired, and tall, like his father. They ran with the wind at their backs, up the steps to the cathedral. Mael Muire held the door open, and Eoin ducked in under his arm. For a moment they stood together in the dark nave, listening to the wind blow under the arched rafters, around the seraphims' burnished wings of oak and flowing gilded robes.

Mael Muire was asleep in his bed.

The Viking ship moved into the north channel of the Shannon just before midnight, as the river went dark. The boat came quickly, all fifty oars dipping and pressing the water back. Her keel moved high above the riverbed. She passed the small church that stood invisible in the dark at the entrance of Lake Derg. As she came onto the open lake, her sails caught the full blast of the wind. A man with a bronze helmet felt the water; the waves ran warm, and then cold into his palm. He called instructions to the helmsman. The dragon shifted left, flanking the current. She followed the cold stream ten miles across the lake, sailing blind around the point, the island, and straight into the narrow entrance of the upper Shannon.

The dragon's head arched right, left, and right again, past the ruins of an ancient ring-fort, past Clonfert abbey, sacked and burned one year before by the Irish king, past the carved stone Clonfinlough on the Pilgrim's Road, moving fast towards Clonmacnoise at the ford of the meadows, the richest monastery in Ireland.

When the moon came out of the clouds, the shape of the river and the banks was revealed. The silver-scaled river wound in and out of the pines; the wind bent their new points back like blades of grass. The trees began to thin out. Then the white stone cap of the watchtower appeared through the trees on the right bank, and the helmsman gave a low whistle. Oars stopped; the ship drifted slowly into the next bend.

Meadows opened up on both sides and the river was a silver flood. The stone buildings of Clonmacnoise were dark. Ropes swung, crossed and fell; the sails drooped. Oars came out and down, quietly gripping the shallows. There was a hush as she came up on the grass, and a rattle of iron swords sliding into bronze scabbards. The dragon nodded as men left her. Five stayed behind to guard the ship.

The Vikings went quickly up the steps and disappeared among the dark buildings. The courtyard was deserted, and for a time nothing happened. Then a light appeared in the last window of the cathedral, near the sacristy. A dog barked; it stopped then started again and kept barking. The light in the cathedral moved from the window to the arched doorway, flared and went out. A few minutes later, an alarm rang out of the tower. Now there were Vikings and white robed men running in the dark. There were shouts and the clash of weapons.

A group of Vikings approached the ship, bearing torches, escorting a dark-haired priest, his homespun robe covered with blood, his hands bound behind him. Two Vikings followed, carrying a man whose arms swung loose and stroked the wet grass. They laid him out gently on the deck beside his helmet and a sack which spilled out silver plates and gold cups, and books with jeweled covers. The young priest dropped to his knees on the grass. He closed his eyes and whispered, "Domine patris..."

A Viking guard watched him. "What's he doing?"

The other shook his head. "I don't know. Perhaps he calls the Fylgja—the spirits of his dead. We found him in the cathedral."

"I don't like it. The wind is changing—the river is not safe. If we stay too long—kill him," said the guard. Then the other man ran a sword through the priest.

Mael Muire was startled out of sleep. He listened for the sound that awakened him; the wind was still blowing hard. He saw the shadow of a tree branch moving back and forth across the stone floor, and turned over. There were stars in the small arched window, and the moon was bright on the limewashed walls of his cell. He remembered that Eoin was in the next room. He closed his eyes and pulled the blanket up over him. Then he heard the dog barking. Probably a strange dog had wandered into the pasture, or maybe, he thought, it was just the storm —dogs sometimes barked at the wind. He stood up, reached for his cloak, and looked out the window. He saw the dragon boat.

He grabbed the knife from the windowsill and ran into

the dark corridor, throwing the door to Eoin's room open. It was empty.

He turned and ran out the side door into the wind. He had to run towards the ship first, then down the steps close to the river to get to the tower, and ring the alarm. The wind was fierce. He slipped going into the second set of steps. Crouching under the stone wall to catch his breath, he looked down at the tower. In the darkness, he could see no one. He pulled his cloak around him, then put his hand on the top of the wall, and started to get up.

There was a man standing on the wall above him. The heel of his boot stopped inches away from the place Mael Muire had put his hand. A blue-tipped sword blade swept the top of his boot, and curved up against his thigh. The man was looking down at the ship. Mael Muire slowly reached inside his cloak and touched his knife handle. The Viking suddenly looked back towards the cathedral. Then he was gone.

Mael Muire bent into the wind and ran down the steps towards the tower.

Near dawn, the first blue light began to burn through the dark. From the slit of window on the top floor of the cloigtheach, Mael Muire saw the dim shape of the hill beyond the river coming, only shape, at first, but then green through the mist. He couldn't see the river, or hear anything but the wind.

There was no smoke in the wind, so he thought the cathedral was unharmed. The tower was stone, except for its wood floors, and the Vikings couldn't burn them out unless they had a ladder and could reach the door. With the wind, they would need shelter to start a fire.

"It's getting lighter, Father," whispered a young monk. "Shall I go down now and see?" Forty men, some wounded, sat huddled in the tower beside a small pile of gold chalices and manuscripts with jeweled covers, waiting for the Abbot's word. No one had seen Eoin.

"Yes," answered Mael Muire. He knotted one end of the rope ladder around an iron hook in the stone wall. The boy wrapped the other end around his waist and his wrist, and went through the trap. They heard him walking on the wood floor below. Then his voice, muffled, "I can't see the boat, I'm going all the way down. Wait for me."

Last night, when Eoin had stretched out on his bed, in the room next to his own, Mael Muire had seen a sword lying under the bed, the heavy twisted bronze hilt sticking out. Was it there when he had looked into the empty room? He couldn't remember. Eoin was a light sleeper; he always woke the moment someone came into his room. Surely the dog had wakened him. But there was no window in Eoin's room; he wouldn't have seen the boat until he got outside. Had he tried to get to the watchtower to ring the alarm, or had he run to the cathedral first, to save the treasures of Clonmacnoise?

"Father Abbot!" The boy's voice was different, calling from the grass below, outside the tower. "Come down. They're gone."

II

"Whence are you, learning's son?"
'From Clonmacnoise I come;
My course of studies done
I am off to Swords again."
"How are things shaping there?"
"Oh, things are keeping fair;
Foxes round churchyards bare
Gnawing the guts of men."

10th-century Irish
trans. Gerard Murphy, *Early Irish Metrics*, Dublin 1961

Mael Muire stood beside the stone called Clonfinlough in open pasture, his horse grazing a short distance away. He had ridden for two hours along the Pilgrim's Road from Clonmacnoise. Not since Eoin's murder, since the raid one year past, had he traveled alone. He and Eoin had always stopped at Clonfinlough on their way east. He traced the white lichen on the massive boulder with his fingers, remembering. The boy had always asked him the same questions, never tired of the answers.

"Tell me about the rock," he always began. "What's this, here?" He stood up on the rock and put his foot in the shallow depression.

"The mark of St. Ciaran's foot, Eoin, when he stood on the rock and spoke with the angels."

"Look, my foot is almost the same size now!"

"Almost."

"And these? Whose footprints are these, father?" Eoin climbed up to the back of the rock, and stretched his foot out beside a narrow trough.

"That's where the angel himself stood, and gave St. Ciaran his powers."

"And this?" Eoin waved his hand over the spreading lichen.

"A map of the ancient world."

"And this thing here, what's this?"

"That's the mark of the giant's child, the Firbolg's son, who scratched his name into the rock, a thousand years before you were born. And those cup marks—"

"—are his thumbprints, where he stuck his thumb that got nettle-burned into the dew on the stone to cool it. I had nettles on my hand, too, father. Don't you remember?"

Mael Muire touched the cup marks; the rough granite was warm. He walked around the boulder, and then he saw the Viking runes. They were new scars in the face of Clonfinlough: "Torbjor owns this rock," he read. He stepped back from the stone and looked at the grass. Only cattle hoofprints showed in the turf, but it had rained last night. The enemy could be nearby. During the past year he had thought of nothing else, but he had no wish to meet Vikings before his journey to St. Kevin's was accomplished. It was two days' ride to Kildare, and then one more to St. Kevin's at Glendalough in the Wicklow Mountains, to return the illuminated psalter that Eoin had made and brought, on the day of the raid, to show him. He led his horse quickly out the woven gate. It started to rain. He rode close to the gorse hedge with his hood pulled down, heading east where light was breaking from the clouds.

There was a fair below the abbey of Kildare, under the watchtower. Mael Muire rode into the crowd of people, sheep, cattle, horses and pigs, over muddy grass and around the booleys, the woven rush huts. He gave his horse to a boy to take up to the abbey, and walked past the turf sellers, the egg sellers, and the men with thatching and reaping tools. He passed the poteen sellers, and the bookmakers, and a young man singing with a band of pipes, drum and harp. Children crowded around the small pen where a woman inside bathed a huge pig with milk, and a litter of striped cats lapped up the drops from the ground. There was a shed with ropes of garlic and leeks hanging from the rafters, and a row of kettles fragrant with nettles, mushrooms and lamb.

Mael Muire had a glass of warm mead from one place, and a loaf of dark oat bread from another. He walked by the cattle and donkeys offered for sale or trade, and tried several knife handles from a shed where a tall, thin man with dark hair was stooped over a long table, arranging his wares. There were twenty smooth stones with holes in them laid out on a cloth, charms for ease in childbirth, healing, and for luck in marriage. There was a piece of flat, weathered limestone with teethmarks along one edge. Mael Muire picked it up.

"That's an ogam stone," said the man, moving down the table. "It's druid writing. Each letter has the powers of a kind of tree. A druid could suffocate a man that was in another county by pressing his own face into a mass of oak leaves and speaking the man's name out loud. That's a rare piece; the only one I've ever seen myself. It belonged to my great-grandmother. My great-grandfather was a druid."

"Maybe he was," said Mael Muire softly, "but that's not ogam, it's a piece of dial; an old sundial."

"Well now, if you're so interested in old things maybe you'd like to see a real treasure." He turned away and came back with a small doeskin package. He opened it and laid it down on the table. There were two dark blue marbles, a silver comb and a shred of skin with some yellow hair attached. "From the grave of a Viking princess. Three men were killed taking these, the fourth got away, and he made me pay a fortune, though some might not have the courage to keep them. But they say a witch's eyes are a powerful charm, and maybe a priest could have use for them. The comb alone is worth the price of a donkey, but for a holy man like yourself, I could do better." He paused and looked at the abbot. "Where are you traveling, Father?"

"To St. Kevin's."

"In the Wicklow Mountains? They're full of Vikings."

"I know my way through the mountains; I was born there."

"Do you have family there?"

He shook his head. "They're gone. Dead." He put a small coin on the table. "For the dial," he said. The man nodded and Mael Muire stuck the rock in his cloak pocket, and turned away into the crowd.

He walked along the muddy path at the edge of the fair, where the racehorses were pacing in their tents, and the tinkers were camped in the trees. There was a great oak tree at the edge of the tinkers' camp. Two light-haired children, a boy about four and a girl, somewhat older, were chasing each other through the trees. The sky was clearing off and the blue Wicklow Mountains were faint on the horizon. At the edge of the woods a blacksmith had set up his forge out of the wind. The man had pale hair, almost white, with his face blackened from ash. He was hammering a wide sword, and red sparks were flying off into the grass. There was a table set before the forge with finished work laid out: three knives and an axe. Two carved bellows leaned against the table. Mael Muire picked up one of the knives. It had a heavy handle, with bands of interlace, a coiled serpent, and the coils were crossed by masses of intricately knotted rope. The handle was made entirely out of silver. It had a good thrusting weight. The abbot asked "How much?" and the blacksmith shook his head. Mael Muire laid down two pieces of silver. The big man nodded and Mael Muire put the knife inside his belt. Then the blacksmith opened his mouth. He spoke the Viking language, the sounds of choking, and cursing. The two children Mael Muire had seen running by the tinkers' camp ran past him, brushing his robe, making the same sounds.

It was late morning when he reached the foothills of the Wicklow Mountains. A granite slab lay flat in the grass between the roots of an old beech tree. He brushed away the dirt and leaves. The stone map showed all the paths through the mountains: the open trails wide enough for a herd of sheep or cattle, and the hidden roads, where a man could travel without being seen. A chiseled circle and stem at the bottom of the map stood for the beech tree. He traced the line, a stream that snaked right and left through the woods towards the mountains. Trees and even the rivers could change in ten years, but the shapes of mountains remained constant. Three mountains and then the vale of Glendalough. The ground was rising under his finger, woods changing from rowan to birch to pine, with glimpses of fields opening up on each side.

He kept climbing. The hills were getting steeper, but they seemed shallow and dry compared to his memory of them. There was too much light; they were too bare and open. Nothing moved until an eagle dropped over the stream. He kicked his horse. They were too visible.

Then the path made a sharp turn. The stream moved off left, and he knew that it wound back slowly and emptied out in the plain above the sea. Before him was a dense pine forest. Somewhere in the woods was the beginning of the pass that led over the three mountains. The way to Glendalough was closed with high brush and pine boughs; he found it and led his mare through. The narrow pass climbed out of the pines, following the turns of the mountain. There was only a low hedge of gorse between him and the valley below. The sun came out and the gorse blazed yellow. An enormous rock loomed over the path on his left, with a trickle of water running down its face into the heather. There were more gigantic boulders ahead. As he passed, he remembered their faces from childhood: the one-eyed giant, the hunchback, and the two-headed trolls.

Somewhere in the valley a bird sang out; a long, low, suspended note and then a high, flutelike flourish that he remembered. He turned again and the three mountains rose up before him; the last was shrouded in fog. The first mountain was rounded, green and dotted with sheep. That meant the Vikings hadn't been here, unless it was their own flock. The sheeps' faces looked thicker and sweeter, different from those in the west.

The second mountain, the red-faced mountain, was straight ahead now. Here there was no cover; the mountain was covered in scorched heather. He headed the horse towards the trees below the third mountain and let her break into a canter. As he rode into the woods he looked up at the third mountain with gigantic rake marks on its face, and the mist pouring over the top. The pass was steep. On both sides of the path were hundreds of little falls, water collecting in the soaked heather and moss and dripping off the burnished mica rocks and the green walls of the glen. Finally, he saw a break in the pines ahead. There, behind the brilliant green wedge of pasture in the center of the gap, rose St. Kevin's tower.

Mael Muire and Abbot Tadg walked around the corner of St. Kevin's cathedral. The wind came up and the air was full of ash floating down from the charred roof beams. Mael Muire stopped by a stone basin outside the gate and dipped his hand in. The tips of his fingers were blackened with a film of ash. They crossed the bridge. Downstream a scorched henhouse lay half in and out of the water, the roof crushed in and the door by itself a few feet away on the wet stones. They walked down to the lake, towards the small chapel of St. Ciaran, where Eoin had been priest. The wind was blowing hard and making white crests on the water.

Tadg bent his head down and entered the low door of the chapel. Mael Muire followed him inside. The chapel was still and dark except for a pale green glow on the stone walls, where the lichen thrived. Mael Muire stood in the middle of the room with his hand on the strap of his satchel. He faced the door; a glint of the lake below came through the trees.

"May I have the book?" Tadg asked softly.

Mael Muire turned the bronze latch on the satchel and removed the manuscript in its soft leather cover. Tadg laid the book on the altar and wrapped it in coarse linen. "There are some things of Eoin's," he said. "The Vikings left this chapel alone."

Mael Muire knelt on the floor and unwrapped the bundle wrapped in Eoin's old brown cloak. Inside was a small harp, a hunting knife with a handle of yew, and a silver traveling paten case. He touched the harp and asked Tadg, "Is there someone here who would play this?" Tadg said, "Yes, a student of Eoin's," and took the instrument. Mael Muire put the paten case on the altar. He stuck the knife under his belt, and folded the robe over his arm.

Later that evening, in the sacristy of the cathedral where Mael Muire was preparing to say mass, Tadg brought him a scrap of vellum, a note from the abbey of Tamlacht, north of the mountains, near the coast. "Come at once to Tamlacht. Breon," it read.

"It came four days ago for you," said Tadg. "But there are Vikings on the river, and in the hills above the Liffey. Will you go?"

"Yes. Breon and I are old friends, collaborators."

"Yes, I remember. You were students here, together. Can you help me with this? It's stuck; everything's damp since the raid."

Mael Muire jerked hard on the drawer in the heavy oak trunk and it came out.

"See if there's a silk stole in there."

He looked through the thin black cassocks, the white, neatly folded albs, the bundles of flax ropes with tassels tucked in. He could smell the satin mixed with cedar, but he came to the end of the drawer; there was nothing else. He took off his brown traveling cloak and put Breon's note inside the inner pocket. Tadg handed him the plain stole; Mael Muire kissed the pale cross on the center seam, then draped it over his neck.

He took cruets of water and wine from a recess in the sacristy, and laid them with a linen napkin on a tray. A boy entered with a torch and caught the oil lamp above the sacristy door. Above the roofless stone walls, there were dark purple streams of clouds passing out from behind the mountain, like currents in the sea.

25

On the morning of Eoin's ordination for the priesthood at Glendalough, Mael Muire said mass. Eoin knelt in the first bench in the nave. Mael Muire stood at the altar, facing the east window with its sharp stones like teeth, and a brilliant white cloud moved into the arch, curling like a fist. He thought, "This is the power and justice of God, the cloud in the wilderness, that no one is safe, not even Eoin on this day, and it is cause for joy."

There was dark in the window above the altar when the boy lit the candles, and Mael Muire put his hands on the polished hewn edge of the altar and knelt down before it.

Speaking the service quietly, he ran the words together, stopping only for the responses. He concentrated on the space beyond the candle glow, speaking and kneeling to the dark that fell away from the altar and reached up into the burnt, arched rafters. He poured wine and mixed it with water. He smoothed the cloth with his hand on the last word of the Sanctus. Then, raising the chalice above his head with both hands he opened his eyes and looked beyond the altar.

Eoin's body was stretched out on a rough table. Crumpled, red-stained rags had fallen away from the dark wounds in his side.

In an instant the dark was empty again, and deep; Mael Muire felt fear pass over him like a winter wave. He set the chalice straight down onto the napkin and stepped back.

The altar boy looked up from his bench. Mael Muire knelt down again, and with both hands raised the chalice above the altar. "I am nothing, I am nothing," he thought, breathing slowly. Aloud, he said, "We are not worthy so much as to gather up the crumbs under Thy Table, but Thou art the same Lord, whose property is always to have mercy..."

"Be careful, Mael Muire, of the Vikings. Nior thug Dia ciall don bhruid," whispered Tadg in the dark at the edge of the lake the next morning. God did not grant reasoning powers to the beasts.

Mael Muire rode north towards Tamlacht, keeping the river on his left as he climbed. He took the steep track above the valley that came out back of the falls. The mist broke up and the sun filled the bottom of the arrow-shaped vale. Branches fell away behind him like bright green water, and there was the sudden sound of water ahead and below him.

"Glenmacnass is full," he said aloud. "I haven't seen the falls for forty years, and they're *full*."

The path to the top of the falls was clear. Deer used it; when he was a boy he'd watched deer come up at dusk to drink from the river in late spring. Badgers and elk crossed the rocks in summer when the falls were down. Once he'd seen a wolverine with eyes like burning pins drinking fast, but he'd never seen a man. Now his white mare drank from a low place on the riverbank, as he knelt beside her, his back to the woods. He looked behind him once; he looked at the deep ferns, at the willow fronds, and at the rowan trees. Nothing moved. He dipped his hands in the river and drank slowly. The river tasted like snow. He watched his hands turn blue in the water.

When he was ten his family had left the mountains. On the last day he went to Glenmacnass: the place where he often sat alone, watching the valley from the top of the falls. That day he climbed down past the granite ledge—the farthest he'd ever gone—past the first drop.

27

He took a red speckled rock with moss on one side right out of the falls. He swore to return some day, when he had power over his life. To seal the oath he put something under the ledge: his talisman, a small piece of iron, with featherlike marks, like ogam, the druid writing. And if he never came back for it, it would be a sign that his life was wrong, a betrayal.

He took his hands out of the stream, rubbed them red on Eoin's cloak, and tied his horse up to a hazel thicket. Then he cut himself a walking stick.

He tossed the head of the willow stick in his hand until the feel of it matched his grip. "I should have brought Eoin up here," he said aloud, and put his stick into the river. He tried a broad, flat stone with the tip of his boot. It wobbled; he stepped on the next one, not so flat but steadier, and in a few minutes was more than halfway to the granite ledge. Then a stone sank down when he stepped on it. He leaned on the willow stick with the water moving fast around his boots. There was no possible rock within reach; he was stranded. There was a flash of red in the rowan trees beyond the hazel thicket, and for an instant Mael Muire saw a blood-tipped Viking spear pinned to the gray bark. But it was only a red bird. His foot slipped and he went down on one knee into the river.

He got up slowly and the red bird flew off. He slammed the stick into the woods, and walked the rest of the way in and out of the water.

The granite ledge was surrounded by swirling water. And he saw what had never occurred to him, in forty years, that nothing hidden at the base of the rock could have survived. Even if the river had been low, what could distinguish between his treasure and the debris of forty years? He climbed up.

There, at the deafening break of water, the top of the spill, he could see far across the glen—to the other side of the world, the Wicklow Mountains going back and back until they were only shapes. Or clouds. The river below was an illogical jumble, just blue places in the pines. It was difficult to connect them.

He stacked four hazel twigs, balancing poles and beams against each other, and made a roof with a large leaf. Two green hazelnuts could rest on the roof with impunity; could one more lie beside them? He lowered a third down onto the leaf with a shaking hand, and the thing collapsed. He swept the fragments with his hand into the falls.

He put his legs out over the edge of the rock. The wind was strong. He looked behind him, at the bare slope. This was how an animal felt in the open. Sunlight moved over the bottom of the valley and the river was a flash of emerald, a green light in the bottom of a deep well. Everything was still except the thundering water. He never saw birds at Glenmacnass. There were always birds on the Shannon River, cranes and kingfishers and geese. He and Eoin had seen a blue heron take off right before them the day the Vikings came.

The first Viking ship he'd ever seen was a wreck off the headlands of Bray. He remembered running to the circle of people, all of them excited and talking loud, and finally getting through the wall of legs. There, in the wet sand, was the head of a monster with red eyes, gold skin and blunt teeth. It reminded him of looking at something else; something that might have been a memory, or a dream or just something he had once been told. A bonfire and blowing leaves, a horse's head with its eyes staring white, and his mother wrapping him in a big blanket and carrying him off to a strange bed.

Once from the tower at Clonmacnoise he watched a ship come from a long way off. The red, wind-billowed sails came first, like a heart beating, turning and twisting on the land as the river twisted and turned. Then the dragon came, with red fire behind its head, with fire for wings, and its head turning to look left and right, looking as the river turned and flowed to find them. That was the day he saw a child scream and cover her ears because the sound she was making frightened her.

He reached into his cloak pocket for the piece of sundial; it fit exactly into his palm. He tossed the stone out over the falls.

There was a challenge he used to give himself, as a child: if he stood up at the edge of the falls and jumped, he might fly to the distant mountain and cloud. In that strange land he would be given a dangerous task. If he believed—it was possible. Perhaps when he had finished someone would come and tell him that Eoin was alive.

He touched the hilt of his knife and started to Tamlacht.

The sky was overcast when he reached Sally Gap, the highest pass in the mountains. He could see Partholon Hill from there. The abbey of Tamlacht stood on the other side of the hill, facing the sea. Two roads led down from Sally Gap to Tamlacht and the sea. One hooked left through dense woods of oak, beech and rowan, the other climbed the turf fields above the river where the drooping cedars ended and the heather was coarse and stunted. He took the road made by the turf carts into open ground.

At the top of Partholon Hill, the ancient plague burial grounds, it began to snow. He guided his horse around the graves. Some were collapsed and others whole under mounds of long dead grass. The jutting slabs of limestone looked more like waves than earth. He decided that it was too dangerous to ride, so he got off his horse and let her go. As he stood brushing the snow off his cloak, he saw three Vikings appear at the edge of the hill.

They're too big for those horses, he thought. The riders weren't moving. He spoke the word, "Amen," but the word curled, darkened and fell flat. Light and snow fell continually; "Amen" would not rise. He touched the knife hilt inside his cloak, and crouched down in a grave. The snow fell faster, and the wind was blowing hard. Now the Vikings had his mare. He laid the Viking knife on the stone in front of him. "We have to be still until we see them coming, Eoin," he whispered, then loneliness came down on him, like a sharp awl, and it shook him. He thought, it will pass, but instead, it grew, like a lake filling up fast. He hugged Eoin's robe around him.

An owl flew past his head; he waved his arm to brush it away. Snow was covering the Vikings, and he was glad. "Eoin," he said to that place in his chest just under the ribs, where his son was now, "I see them coming," he whispered.

He picked up the knife and left the shelter, bracing himself against the wind. The riders were close; he could see the horses' feet plunging up and down in the snow. Suddenly the snow was blowing from all directions and a horse was on top of him. He was knocked down. He was turning around and around inside the white wave and he couldn't find the top to break through and breathe—his lungs would soon burst with snow. Then he felt the ground under him. He looked up and there was a Viking, bringing his sword around like a scythe looking for wheat. The sword passed him, tarnished with a black stain halfway up the jagged blade. Mael Muire grabbed the Viking's leg and shoved the knife into it. The horse lunged forward and he fell again. There was a shrill scream, and another, and a word—"Fylgja!"—hanging in the snow.

Before he opened his eyes, he knew that the Vikings were gone. It was quiet; the wind had dropped. Lying on his back in the snow, he looked at a band of light under the heavy clouds; the glow was spreading. He turned onto his side.

There was a man standing on the high mound at the edge of the hill. He was carrying a long spear made of ice, and his helmet was made of ice; Mael Muire could see the dark cloud through it. Then a group of men, women and children, dressed in white, came up behind him, until the edge of the hill was lined with people.

Mael Muire got up. He pulled Eoin's cloak tight around him and started walking. When he reached the north edge of the hill, the clouds were beginning to break up. The snow melted away under his boots. He kept the lights of Tamlacht before him and started down the hill.

III

*"Never before has such a terror come
As we have now suffered from the Vikings
Nor was it ever thought that such an inroad
From the sea could be made."*

Lindisfarne Journal, 793

The shepherd's path came down from the mountain, ran along the stone pasture, passed the high tower and came to an end at the stable. Breon's cell was beyond, the last on the north end of the abbey. Snow had drifted away from the mountain side of the path, like a thick white rope. Two whitefaced cows slept under a stone wall; a murder of crows was still in a bay tree, its leaves still tightly curled, shiny and dark over the snow. The evening was getting warmer. Mael Muire took three steps for every breath. The sound of breathing was loud on the path. He knew he was getting close to the door—the dark place in the low, white wall—when it opened and he was stopped by a flood of light.

A man bent his head under the arch. Breon with his beaked nose and thick eyebrows peered out. "Who is it? Mael Muire?" He grabbed his shoulder. "Come inside. My God, I'd given you up. Things have been bad, here. Snow, this late. It's been dark all day. You didn't see anything, did you?"

Mael Muire shook his head, and sat on a bench by the fire.

"Dinner's coming soon. River salmon." Breon's black and white sheepdog got up from under the table and clicked across the stone floor to the bench. She pushed her nose under Mael Muire's hand. He rubbed her head and took a glass of mead from Breon.

"I heard you were alright. Last summer, after the raid. I didn't know about Eoin until later. I'm so sorry...."

"I know." That feeling of unreality started to come back, and he felt for the knife under his cloak. It was gone.

"This year, they will destroy us. First day the mist rises—the ships come. Good Friday it was. Andrew put our chalice down the well; but they never came. We counted sixty ships before dark." He took a brush out of his pocket and called the dog. She stood still by his knee as he brushed her. "What are they going to do with sixty ships?"

"What they do with one," said Mael Muire, coming to the table. He decided to say nothing to Breon about the mountain. He couldn't explain what had happened, or answer his questions; luckily there was no blood on him. He still had the feeling that something was going to happen—something unstoppable, like an earthquake, or a thunderstorm. He filled his glass.

"Some of the people here have started selling them winter corn. I've seen Viking patterns on cloth and cups." Breon stood up and tossed a branch into the fire. "If they deal with Vikings, they're better off dead. Where is that boy? How long does it take to cook a fish?" He opened the door that led to the main hallway and looked out. "I don't know what he's doing."

"St. Kevin's suffered in the raid," said Mael Muire. Breon was too preoccupied to notice anything; besides, they were both tired. "Tadg is leaving—he's going to Brittany this summer."

Breon shrugged.

"You could go too."

He closed the door. "I'm too old to run away. Mael Duin was an old man when the Vikings came the first time to Tamlacht. It must have been bitter to see them destroy what he had made. But when he built Tamlacht he said, 'Anyone who deserts his country except to go from the east to the west and from the north to the south is a denier of Patrick in Heaven and of the faith in Erin.'"

"Mael Duin didn't have sixty Viking ships in the bay beyond," said Mael Muire.

Breon sat down and poured himself another glass of mead. "We don't know that. It was fifty years ago." He watched the fire. "Mael Duin only fasted three times. That was against the pagan king Artri who had powerful magic. After the first fasting the king's leg broke in two, after the second the fire fell out of the hearth and burned him from head to foot and after the third fasting he died.

"I've spent my life studying his Rules. But I can see no magic in them. The model ascetic life—he invented it—no music, no meat, no women, every moment of waking filled with prescribed prayer." He shook his head in disgust. "Self-denial is no weapon. There must be something else, something he never spoke about... something he couldn't write down. A powerful kind of knowledge, a weapon to use against Vikings.

"No one goes against them. We don't believe they can be stopped. But Mael Duin didn't know fear himself—he had the power to destroy an enemy, and when I find out what it was, then Christians will understand how wrong it is to be afraid, to pretend to friendship with the enemy. In time the monasteries will be full of young men again. Glendalough and Clonmacnoise will be what they once were. Young men like Eoin will have a chance to do good work of their own." He was silent; he got up and put a piece of turf on the fire.

Mael Muire looked into his glass. He turned it slowly in his hand and the liquid inside came up closer and closer to the rim, like a wave on a flooding riverbank. He put the glass down.

Breon walked up and down the room. "He had more followers than St. Patrick, and he changed the monastic life in Ireland and in all of Europe forever. But there's nothing about his youth, his family—no reference to his spiritual conversion—no real clues of any special ability. Nothing. Until now. I want to show you something."

He laid two pages on the table. "I told you that Andrew dropped the chalice down the well. We had to go down there and get it out. We found something; a box stuck into a space between two rocks. It's an old letter from before the first raid—"

April 25, 792 Tamlacht.

Dear Tomas,

I hope you are well. The storm was bad here. We lost two cows, and the thatch off the barn. But something else has happened. Mael Duin has left us. Before Matins I went down to the river to check the curragh. Three days ago I beached the boat high on the rocks, weighted it down with stones as the Abbot taught me. No wind or wave moved it. I could see where the keel made a straight furrow in the sand, as he'd dragged it into the river.

Last night I made up his fire as usual after evensong. It was dark and at first I didn't see him. He was standing by the open window. Rain was pouring in, his eyes closed, his cassock drenched. He said come here, and he put a box in my hands. He said, keep this safe for me. Someday a man will come for it. His name is Diuran Leccerd; the half-poet. He's not a Christian, but a druid, and you must give him this for me. He smiled and told me there was nothing to be afraid of. He gave me his blessing and told me to go.

It is now past midday. The bells have rung one hour. Someone has ridden from the river and his horse dropped dead in the courtyard. The brothers have gone up into the hills. Mael Duin will not be alone this day. His treasure is with me here. I have thought this hour about a hiding place. It's big enough for this book and the box. The Vikings won't get them. Pray for us, Tomas. Pray for us, Father.

Mael Muire laid the two pages carefully down on the table and rubbed his eyes. Breon took a rough wood box out of his trunk and placed it on the table between them.

"What is it, a reliquary?" asked Mael Muire.

"No. You're the pre-Christian scholar. This is something in your area. Take a look."

Mael Muire opened the box. He took out a piece of silver net, and gently turned it over in the lamplight.

"It has the color of silver but not the feel, and what silver gives off that kind of light?" asked Breon.

"What is it?" Mael Muire smoothed it flat on the table. His hand shook.

"I don't know. I don't like to touch it. I've never seen anything like it. Some piece of clothing or ritual adornment— some disgusting pagan ritual object."

"It's beautiful."

"What matters is that I have the bait that will get me information."

"The druid? Diuran Leccerd? He must be dead, Breon; what can he tell you now?"

"He's not dead; he's coming here, tonight." Breon put his hands together, speaking rapidly. "They were boys together and they went to sea. They were gone a long time, and given up for dead—but I've found him and he's agreed to make a trade. He's promised to talk to me about Mael Duin and I'm going to give him the thing that he thought was lost—this...treasure."

"Breon, there are no living druids...the man would have to be well over a hundred—"

"Wait; listen to me. Do you remember the summer we went to Kerry—you were looking at sundials in Daingan —and the bishop of Munster told me about the curragh builder who was supposed to be a relative of Mael Duin's?"

"Yes, I remember—he lived on Blasket Island, you went out there, and he told you nothing."

"His name was Diuran. A huge man. He had a boy working with him. He said he'd never heard of Mael Duin and went back to work. But I saw the boy look at him. He knew something and he knew not to tell.

"How can we accept the acts of Patrick and Brigid and doubt the possibility of miracles in our own time? I'm an old man, Mael Muire, with my enemy about me. There's no time left to fall in love or wait for luck to place my enemy in my power. There's so much to find out, so much of importance." He shook his head, and his dog put her head under his hand.

It had stopped snowing. The grey horse shook his mane with a spray of snow. The riders pulled up, and for the first time that night saw their own shadows, blue on the brilliant ground. A full moon was up; before them a stand of white birches rose on the hill. Black birds flew out of the trees without a sound. The boy said, "It's so quiet."

His rope slackened; the grey horse galloped up the rise, then stopped. The man beside him pulled back the hood of his cloak and looked away into the dark east. The boy came up beside him.

"We're almost there. Do you hear the sea?"

The boy listened. "No, Diuran."

"No. You'd be swimming before you heard anything. Don't worry, we go north here. Look for the Round Tower, we should begin to see it over the next rise. I don't know why we can't see it now, especially with this moon." He sighed. "The woods have grown thicker. Let's go."

There was a knock at the door and Breon opened it. His servant entered and placed a platter of cheese, broiled fish and oatcakes next to Mael Muire's elbow. They ate in silence. Mael Muire divided the last oatcake between them. Breon put the platter down for the dog.

Mael Muire walked to the hearth. He laid branches in one by one, tucking turf and thistles into the cold black spaces between the logs. He stood, and with a small movement of his staff, the hearth boomed and lit up the corners of the cell. "Still," he said suddenly, "there's no one who can tell why Mael Duin left Tamlacht that morning—"

"No; that's true. I think he left the abbey to risk a confrontation on his own with the Vikings. What was it he said to his disciples? 'The fire you most dread to burn you, to it shall you go.' "

Mael Muire said nothing.

Diuran and the boy led their horses down the cattle track. The round tower was between them and the low monastery. Beyond the last building, the world dropped off. In the east a ragged edge of silver marked the distant breakers.

Diuran whispered, "Now do you hear it?" The boy shook his head. As they passed beneath the tower the boy looked up. The moon peered over the roof above the single empty window—the blind eye. They walked on, stopping at the last building.

"This was Mael Duin's room; the last window that looks on the sea. Hold my horse and wait for me." Diuran walked to the window and looked in. On the left wall he saw a stone hearth, the fire low. On the opposite side of the room two monks sat at a long table. The younger man, with close-cropped black hair, he didn't know. The other, thin and older with heavy eyebrows, he had met. On the table under his right hand was the box. Diuran's own hand went automatically to the frozen mica in the window. His long fingers caught an aurora on their edges from the firelight. He put his hands inside his cloak and drew away.

There was a light knock on the door. Mael Muire and Breon looked at each other. Breon rose from the table. Mael Muire's hand went to his staff as the door opened. In the dark hall stood Brother Sean, pale, with a candle in his hand. "There are two travelers to see you, Father," he whispered.

Breon's back straightened. "Tell them to come in, then go to bed. I'll call you if I need anything."

Mael Muire walked to the fire and put another log on it. He straightened the blanket on the cot. When he turned around, they were standing in the doorway: a tall man and a boy behind him.

The man's yew stick was level with his eyebrows, which were black and straight with a slight lift at the end like clipped arrow feathers. His hands were remarkable. The long fingers of one curled around the stick delicately; the other hand rested against the ash door frame and it seemed to have grown from the ash tree itself.

"You are Abbot Breon, then," he said.

"Yes. It's been many years, hasn't it? I remember the boy, I think. His red hair. Would you like some wine? This is my friend, Mael Muire, abbot of Clonmacnoise."

"Father," Diuran nodded and smiled slowly.

Mael Muire pressed his hand. "Diuran. You must be tired. I myself have traveled today, though not so far."

Diuran took off his cloak, laid it beside him on the bench and leaned his back against the table. Mael Muire poured four cups of hot wine. He put one down in front of Diuran, reaching across his immense staff with strokes carved halfway up.

"That's ogam, isn't it?" said Breon, watching the two men.

Mael Muire glanced at the big man, then stared into Breon's eyes as he spoke casually to his friend. "Quite unusual...the church made bonfires of them two hundred years ago. A druid's ogam staff is his memory; each group of marks stands for a poem."

"I've seen the marks on pillars in the west," said Breon.

"Would you like to see my staff?" Diuran gave a cup of wine to the boy. "Go stand by the fire, Aed Finn, you're shivering." The boy hung Diuran's cloak on a nail by the fire to dry. Mael Muire could smell the sea in it, and smoke.

Breon nodded to Mael Muire, and glanced towards the pine box. Mael Muire could see that he considered the staff a safe hostage in his hands until the big man gave up his information.

Mael Muire took the staff and sat on the bench by the hearth. He turned it slowly in the firelight. It looked real enough; at worst it was an excellent fake. There wasn't enough time to decipher it all, but he could begin. If he could make out a phrase he might begin to establish a regional history, at least, something to suggest authenticity. Old fishermen or boatbuilders from the southwest didn't read the ogam. He began where the strokes ended, in the middle of the staff, the last phrase carved.

Yes, he thought, there was the complete phrase, marked off by a space below. The characters were very worn, so the druid— if there had been a druid—had habitually held his staff at that position. It was interesting that the staff was half-carved. The poet must have died young. The first character was surely the yew mark, five short horizontal cuts on a vertical stem. The yew is a vowel, but which—of course, *i*. This second character was repeated, a diagonal with no stem, therefore a consonant: the vine, *m*. The elder, five diagonals: an *r*—that was easy. Next was another vowel: *a*, the fir; a single horizontal cut across the vowel stem. Here was vine again. So the first word was immram—voyage.

Mael Muire looked up. The boy was gazing at him, sitting cross-legged on the floor. At the table Breon and the big man sat over the manuscript, Breon talking softly. Mael Muire turned to the boy.

"Can you read the ogam?"

The boy shook his head and smiled. "No, Father. I can read Latin. I learn at the bishop's school, winters in Ardfert."

"Ah." Mael Muire ran his hand over the shallow notches: voyage. Three more words. The next one was difficult, the engravings very shallow. There were six characters, all different. Hazel, heath, elder, fir, yew, ivy—Curaig. Curaig was the old form of curragh: boat. Voyage-boat. That made sense. These last two words must be a name. He worked fast now. Each had four letters, no repetitions. Wait a minute—wait a—this was impossible. Vine, fir, aspen, rowan. Next word. First letter: oak. Oak? What was that Breon had said? Not elder, but oak. Then the next was, yes, there it was, heather, then yew. And the last had to be ash. A cold finger traced his spine. Oak, not elder. Immram Curaig Mael Duin. The Voyage of Mael Duin's Boat.

Diuran was looking at him. Mael Muire gave him the staff. "The marks are worn."

"Yes, they are worn." Diuran took the huge staff in his hands and closed his eyes. His fingers moved over the marks. He looked from Mael Muire to Breon. "Shall I read them for you? That is our bargain, isn't it? But first, give me the box."

"I will," said Breon, and he looked quickly at Mael Muire. "But if you don't keep your word I'll fast against you like Patrick did against the druid Cetach."

"You would lose. You'll have to trust me. I'm no stranger to fasting, though not by choice. I know what you do. You starve yourself until you can see the grain in your cell door breathe—until the snakes coil out of the branches outside your window. Then your god speaks from his perch on your wall."

Breon said, "Our founder, Mael Duin, believed that fasting had great virtue."

"Did he? Perhaps. I think, though, that what Mael Duin believed was as great a mystery to you as it was to me."

"You can't possibly understand our life—or what was his. It doesn't matter. Here, take it," said Breon, pushing the box across the table towards him.

Diuran opened the cover and took out the length of silver net. He draped the mesh over the back of his hand. The other, open palm caught up the ends; built up ridges, silver mountains seen far in the distance after rain. He let it all slide down into his open hand; the mountains collapsed into waves. He closed his hand. "It's true. He's gone." He dropped to his knees. He pressed the silver against his face and rocked. A deep moan came out of him; it grew and waned with the rhythm of his rocking. He's not a fraud, thought Mael Muire, he's a madman. When Diuran stood up again his face was clear, as though he'd just wakened from a long sleep.

"I'm no druid," he said. "Tell your friend not to be afraid of me. I learned some poetry long ago; but you see my staff is unfinished. I'm Diuran Leccerd, half-poet. I don't make magic; I make boats, small boats for lakes and shallow bays.

"They say that no man dies but by accident; I believe that. But I've seen too much to believe that a man can order his mind or his actions. Some years the Vikings come. A wolf gets into the cattle. A man goes crazy with hunger and eats his horse, though it is forbidden. His family dies anyway. I've seen a whole lake of dwellings burning.

"But there are always signs, though few these days can read them. When Mael Duin's luck changed, my brother and I went over and over it afterwards. Nobody had seen anything—not even the druid, Nuca—no slanted smoke, no sickness in the cattle, not even a falling star. It was like night and day were turned around. As if mistletoe

44

was for eating and wool for making rope, or as if the secret of iron had never been found, and we used stone only to carve our meat." He paused. "Aed Finn, will you give me something to drink?" Breon pushed a cup and the wine towards him. "Our horses need food and shelter; there is a stable?"

"Yes, beyond the tower," said Breon.

"Will you see to the horses, Aed Finn?"

The boy went out quickly. The three men sat at the table, drinking in silence. When the boy returned, stamping the snow off his boots in the doorway, Diuran refilled his glass.

"We were part of the same family," he began, "the tuath, in Connemara. We grew up together, Mael Duin and his three brothers, my brother Germane and I. When we were Vikings he always made the rules for capture and torture. But he took the whipping when Germane set the thatching stacks on fire. He dreamed up the banshee in the woods, but he taught us to be brave. Mael Duin was the best of us all at games, at learning; but besides that, he was different. He would have been our chieftain. But in the end, the tuath hated him.

"The night before I left my family with the druid Nuca to begin my ollamh study, when I was fourteen and Mael Duin a year older, I was glad when he came away and stayed with me." He smoothed the silver mesh on the table, then took the big staff in his hands.

"Immram Curaig Mael Duin. Ardri uasal Na N-uile. Creator of all things, world-maker, in every time and in every space, help us. Show us first the forms and all appearances. It is no shame to name them. Then teach us how to strip the bark from the tree."

2

I remember that it had been raining hard for a week; the lake was high, and Mael Duin's house had taken in water. His mother, Fedelm, was the chieftain's widow, and their log and wattle crannog guarded the lake at the lowest and most vulnerable point. No Viking or Irish raider had ever crossed the threshold of Lough Corrib, or the door of their crannog; only the brackish water and mud that Mael Duin, my brother Germane and myself had spent all morning sweeping out of the house. By afternoon the lake had stopped rising and was still as glass; the sky was clear and a warm breeze had come up. From the door of Fedelm's crannog I saw her other sons, Cailte, Arden and Seamus, put nets and spears into the curragh and head towards the river. They left us the small lake curragh to do our work from; it was more like a basket than a boat. At dusk they came back trailing three big salmon. They dropped one fish at their mother's door and took the rest to shore to roast.

Germane kept the curragh steady with his pole driven between the roots of the crannog, the great oak piles dug from the bogs in the valley below. I watched the oil lamp that hung on a stick of its own so that Mael Duin could see to weave the thatching sticks, the long willow branches, back in place where the rising water had worked them loose. I handed him thatch and held the knife while he worked along the curved wall.

By the time we passed the fish trap under the back porch of the crannog it was getting dark, later than any of us had ever stayed out alone. The lights in crannogs across the lake went out. The river passageway with its willow shrouds closed up, and then there was nothing at all beyond the circle of light from our lamp. Germane pulled out the pole and we drifted around the wall. He stuck the pole into the mud again and Mael Duin leaned out and grabbed hold of a branch to bring us close. I moved next to him, to balance the boat, and I saw his dark eyes intent and his steady, peat-streaked hands focused in the lamplight. He always looked like that when he was working, and sometimes when he was imagining things; it was one of the things that made him different. Everyone said his looks were more fitting a high king than the chieftain of a small fine of twenty-three crannogs. My mother said his eyes were darker blue than the skies at midsummer and his hair more gold than the hill fires. Fedelm told her once that's why she kept him hidden until he was six months old; so the people of the passage graves wouldn't be jealous and steal him from her.

In those days I didn't have a name for their kind. My father told me that they were the people of the goddess Danu—tall, fair and afraid of nothing but the iron weapons that we, the dark people, brought west with us from some other place. So they hid in the passage graves with their stone weapons and their magic ways until they forgot how to breathe out in the light, or walk straight on earth or swim like men do in the lakes or the sea. There was a grave just beyond the willows where the river comes into the lake, and fifty of them on Rath Cetach above the lake, but I didn't like to think about that when the lake was dark and quiet.

Mael Duin, though he had no choice in the matter, didn't want to be a chieftain, but a hero like Cuchulain, who never turned from battle, and who died young with his horse staying by him until the last drop of blood drained out of his wounds. But I wanted Mael Duin to become a high king, and I believed he would; and I was

going to be his chief poet. My father had at last con-
sented to let me go with Nuca, the druid, and study the
ollamh, and I was to leave my family the very next day.

Mael Duin told me that after Nuca and I left he was
going to look for birch roots for the gunnels of the
curragh he was building. They would come out easily
after the rain. The sky overhead was clear, and almost
black. "The hunter is up," said Mael Duin. "You can see
his shield tonight." He pushed his hair out of his eyes and
leaned back in the curragh. He asked me if I was scared
to be alone with the druid, scared to learn magic and
poetry. I said I was afraid I would be too stupid to learn
magic and poetry and that Nuca would send me home.
Germane said that since I'd have my own horse, maybe I
wouldn't have to come home. Then Arden yelled from
across the lake that we were late, we had to go in. A baby
cried in one of the houses farther in, and a woman cursed
us for making noise. We rowed across the lake to our own
house, and Mael Duin held the curragh against the
tether pole until Germane and I were out. Germane went
inside and I could hear my father growling at him. Mael
Duin slipped his arm bracelet off and put it in my hand.

"Take this with you," he said.

I told him to come back, after his family was asleep, if
he could, and then he rowed away into the dark. My
mother was kneeling at the fire when I went in, but my
father was standing by the door. He took me into his
room, his big hand clutching my shoulder hard. "The
least you could do is spend your last evening at home
with your mother. I don't understand you."

I lay awake long after they all slept, looking at the
shadows from the fire dancing on the domed roof, and
waiting for Mael Duin. When he finally came, I made
room for him on my pallet, and we talked and watched

the stars through the chimney hole. After awhile he turned over on his side. The blanket slipped off his shoulder and more than anything I wanted to put my arm over him and go to sleep. But Mael Duin was a light sleeper and I was afraid to wake him. He must have left before daylight because when I opened my eyes, there was a circle of light blue sky in the chimney hole and he was gone.

The next time I saw Mael Duin I had spent one year with the druid. When Nuca, my father and I made the gesa pact which bound me to him for seven years of study, it was agreed that I would return each spring to help with the planting and thatching, and to stay with the tuath in case of raids. We had to return to the lake by Beltane, the eve of May, and I was glad not to miss the games.

Nuca and I rode south two days before Beltane, through the steep, green fields I had worked summers as a boy. We climbed a hill, and I saw the distant edge of Lough Corrib flex like a sheet of tarnished silver. After walking a year in the rich woods and meadows of the east, the rough looks of the west made my chest hurt. It started to rain and we rode down. The rain made a drum of the pasture, but it was quiet under the trees with a floor of needles. The trees were far apart; our ponies walked easily.

By mid-morning we rode along the salt inlet, the same water that, turning fresh, brings salmon to the door of our crannogs. We stopped at a little pool beside a black, upturned curragh tied to the stones she was resting on, and Nuca found a purple sea urchin. He showed me how to make it expel its orange foam—a good salve, he said, for jellyfish stings, or blistering burns. He found some medicinal plants growing out of the limestone, and decided that we should make a collection.

"They start the games at dusk," I reminded him, and pointed to the sun, which was just breaking over the cliffs. "Yes, it's hot," he replied, and stripped off cloak and shirt. I was sorting petals, stems and leaves when there was a rustle above us and a small avalanche of sand and stone. I grabbed my knife. The strand was empty. A gull screamed and took off; a single cloud was slowly moving east. If the sea urchin could come so far up surely a dragon boat with sloping neck and red sails could navigate the bay. I stared at the cliffs, at the blinding sunlight, and a dark blotch moved above us. I stepped back and there was Mael Duin on a horse, black mane and gold mane standing out in the wind.

"Wait there, I'm coming down," he called and disappeared. In a moment he was cantering along the strand. Nuca gave me a shove on the back. I leapt onto my horse and rode after Mael Duin. Nuca was asleep when we returned, his brown back glistening with salt. We took a swim and pulled up on a ledge that stuck out over the water.

"You don't look any different," said Mael Duin. He picked up a piece of driftwood and scraped away a patch of lichen, then threw the stick into the water. "But when I saw you, on the beach, I didn't know you at first. I only recognized you because of this." He touched the bracelet on my arm. The interlocking arcs of gold matched the torc around his neck. "It's true, Diuran," he said. "I wasn't looking for you. We thought you'd be coming south, through the pass."

It was just luck he had ridden down to the strand. I told him that I'd thought he was a Viking.

He laughed and lay down on his stomach, his cheek on

his folded arms. "I'm sorry to disappoint you," he said. "You could come home with a row of skulls riding on your staff, instead of a sack of pincushions. What are you going to do with them?"

"Use them for burns," I said.

"I'll have my weapons forged this summer," he said. "The elders have decided—I will be chieftain when I turn seventeen." He sighed and turned his head, and the gold neck torc flashed in the sun. "I don't think Ardan minds. He's got the cattle, and he's building a house; he has a lover now. Well, Diuran Leccerd, will you make a poem tonight, at the bonfire?"

I said I wasn't a poet yet, and that I hadn't learned anything except the names of trees and grass.

He said I should be glad I wasn't trapped on the lake. I told him how my uncle on Achill Island in the north said wasn't it strange that I wasn't growing tall, with such big hands and a tall father. He looked disgusted, and buried his face in his arms. We didn't talk for awhile. I lay on my back and looked at three specks of blue sky through the holes in an abalone shell. "What makes these holes? Nuca would know. He knows everything." I passed the shell over to Mael Duin. "Three holes. She puts her marks on things. What was that we used to say casting stones? 'Three for the triple goddess who made the world: the cloud, the wave and the hill.' "

" 'One for the girl, one for the mother and one for the old hag who tricks you and gives you your death.' " We laughed. We talked about the games, and drinking, and then we woke Nuca and rode to the lake.

Once I thought I'd killed Mael Duin on Rath Cetach. It was the winter before his father died in a cattle raid in Sligo. Mael Duin had a yellow cat that followed him around, and when it got sick his father gave him a hammer and told him to take it into the woods and kill it. I kept out of sight behind a big tree, but it was cold and he saw my breath. He didn't say a word, but I saw that his face was wet from tears. He took the cat into the calving shed and shut the door. He must have buried it in the woods, because when I went into the shed later that day there was just a flat place in the straw and the close, sweet smell of hay and dung and warm animals.

He didn't talk to me for a week. He was up on Rath Cetach with all the other boys playing raids. I stood in front of him and he wouldn't look at me. I picked up a big stick and hit him in the head. He lay white and still on the cave floor for a long time. A dark place came up on his forehead. When he woke up he told Germane he'd kill him if he told anyone.

That afternoon Mael Duin took the prizes in horse racing, leaping and running. Germane and I drank three skins of mead, but Mael Duin drank his mixed with water, because of the chess game in the evening. The championship match was held outside, it being so fair, under the stars. Fedelm set up her own gaming table for the match with the silver and coral enameled riders and rooks and chariots. There was a torch set at each corner of the table and two stools with the triple face of the goddess carved on each of three legs. Nuca drew a line with his staff in the dirt ten paces from the table on each side; the tuath had to stay beyond to give the players room to think. Before the draw for pieces Nuca sang a long poem about the game, telling how the lovers Dierdre and Naisi played chess waiting for the jealous King Conchubar's henchmen to break down the door and kill them, and how Amergin, the first poet, had invented the game when his people first came to Erin, to teach them how to wage war against the giants.

Mael Duin took his place at the table, wearing a lapis-colored cloak with gold crescents that Fedelm had made for him. His opponent, an older man with thick gold bracelets, was chieftain from Achill. Nuca put two pawns, silver and coral, in a water jug and gave the guest first draw. He couldn't get his hand to the bottom, his forearms being so thick, so Nuca tipped the jug. The suspense of the moment was wrecked by a sudden loud lowing in the woods, a scramble and delay while some-one who had forgotten to milk his cow broke from the laughing crowd.

Mael Duin checked his opponent in six moves; three more and he killed the king, beating his own record of the previous year by five moves. I brought fresh clothes to the changing tent; even his cloak was soaked through from the effort of the game. Nuca put the silver victor's collar around his neck, and then Mael Duin went outside to the crowd. I folded his clothes over a drying rack above the muddy racing shirt and breeches he'd worn that afternoon. When I turned around, Nuca was standing in front of the door, looking at me.

"He's a lucky young man. What would you trade, Diuran, to be your friend tonight?"

"No one can do what he does," I answered.

"Nor so easily."

The mead was sour in my mouth. "I'll work harder next year, Nuca."

"You'll have to work harder, of course. Next year you'll grow fast, and need more sleep."

The walls of the tent were spinning; I hoped that the cool night breeze on my face might keep me from faint-ing or throwing up.

Nuca was silent, but didn't move away from the door.

Then I heard myself asking, well knowing that I'd have despair for my answer, "If he weren't Fedelm's oldest son, if he didn't have to be chieftain; he would be a great druid... wouldn't he?"

"Go on, get out." Nuca held the flap of the tent away and I ducked under his arm, and ran straight into Germane.

Germane said that Nuca was strange, and that my father thought I was crazy, but that he was glad I was home. We laughed and finished a full wine sack and went back to the shore to see if there was any roast boar left, because Germane was starving.

It was the next day that Mael Duin lost his luck. I woke late that morning with a hammer going in my head. I had to help my father mark off the flat hill for stone throwing and talk to my mother while she baked honey cakes so I only saw Mael Duin once before the games began at noon. My father and I had gone up onto Rath Cetach to pick up good stones; the cave is part of an old barrow and white, fist-sized stones lie everywhere. We didn't talk much. Rath Cetach had an empty feel about it. On the way down we saw Mael Duin on the lake; he waved and called out, "Find me a lucky stone."

There were some young men from the north at the games that year, foster sons of Achill who'd spent the winter in our tuath and would take corn back to their families after the harvest at Samhain. One of them, a tall, red-haired boy with a nervous bay stallion, had come in just behind Mael Duin in the horse race. He was the son of Fedelm's widowed sister who lived in Achill. He and Mael Duin's brothers had gotten drunk together all night and complained about the judges. When my father and I got out on the game hill he was already practicing. Earlier he'd thrown a stone through Fedelm's roof; Ardan spent the morning patching and cursing. When the tuath gathered on the hill, it was only Cailte and Seamus who followed the red-haired boy around. Ardan bet heavily on Mael Duin, and stood by Germane and me saying anybody who bet on red hair was a fool.

Each contestant got three throws, and guests went first. The Achill boy threw two stones that fell a few paces beyond the first mark, but his third throw was lucky and fell just short of the last mark, a row of birches. He turned to the crowd and bowed low. Ardan swore. There was a long delay while more bets were taken. Mael Duin stood in the waiting circle, chewing on a blade of grass. When the last wager had been made he picked up a stone from the pile, took a breath and let it fly. There was a moment when nobody made a sound, then a distant crash, as the stone fell far into the birch glade.

The red-haired boy turned to Mael Duin. "It's not fair; the wind quit when you started."

"I don't know what you're talking about," Mael Duin answered him.

"You know what I mean."

Mael Duin stepped aside and waved at the pile of stones. "Take another turn."

The boy picked up a stone. He looked at Mael Duin and a channel of sunlight passed over them both. The gold torc around Mael Duin's neck skimmed the wave and went under it.

"Bastard," the boy said. His face was red, the skin peeling away from his nose.

Mael Duin said, "The air is dead. Look at the trees below. Take another turn. Take it *now.*"

Then the boy dropped the stone. "Forget it!" He whirled around to the crowd. "Look at the grass, the wind's come up again. It's witchcraft. I'm not stupid. It stinks of rotten magic."

"It was luck," Mael Duin said.

"Luck?" The boy screamed. "What do you think I am, a fool?" He stood still for a moment, then spat on the ground near Mael Duin's feet.

Mael Duin didn't move. Nuca put his hand on my shoulder and I jumped.

"Who are you?" said Mael Duin. "What is your name?"

"You know my name—"

"Where is your father's shield? Your torc?" He touched the gold collar around his neck. "What are you afraid of? The wind? The trees? Me?" Mael Duin laughed. "Don't be afraid. I won't touch you. I've heard that Vikings are afraid of the earth—afraid of men. Where are your father and your brothers? Their skulls ride the mast of a Viking ship. You must have found a good hiding place."

"You never killed a man!" screamed the boy.

"Or loved an enemy."

"The Viking woman? I killed her afterwards. I did myself. She was washing her husband's body, my father's kill—"

"Filth!" Mael Duin turned his back on the boy.

"What do you expect, going against a witch's son? I know about you." He pointed at Fedelm. "You're not her son. Everyone in Achill knows you're a bastard. Ask her. Ask her."

"Shut up!" Ardan yelled, pushing his way through the crowd.

"Why are you sticking up for him? He's not your brother. He's taken your place. It's you ought to be chieftain, instead of cowherd for his cattle—"

"I said shut up!" Ardan hit him in the mouth and knocked him into the grass.

Mael Duin pushed Ardan away and stood over the boy. "Get up. Get up!" The boy got up grinning, a stone in each hand; when he hit the ground, they rolled onto the grass, two flat stones from the cave on Rath Cetach.

Then Fedelm pulled the boy to his feet. "You are a guest of the lake. You may thank the goddess for your life. The keening would be short on your death day. Go into the house and wash yourself. Don't let me see your face again this day."

Mael Duin took his mother's arm and turned her to him. "What are you doing?"

She said, "Let go, Mael Duin. You're hurting my arm."

Mael Duin said, "It's a lie."

"You mustn't fight him."

"It isn't true. Look at me, look at me, Mother."

"You're hurting me."

He let go of her. "Is it true? Mother, is it true?" She closed her eyes. He looked at her face. "You can't deny it, then." He wiped his eyes with the back of his hand. "Who are my parents?" he asked softly.

She shook her head.

"Tell me who I am."

"You are my son; who here will say that you are not? These people know I nursed you and Ardan both in a year of famine. Listen to me, Mael Duin. I know you will believe nothing I say to you now, but forgive us. It's not their fault; not even my husband knew. You came to me starving in a year of hunger."

"Tell me," he said.

"It doesn't matter. You are my foster child. There is no shame in that."

He told her he wasn't a child, that he wasn't afraid. "Tell me before the tuath or I swear a fasting against you."

Still she wouldn't speak. He ripped the gold collar from his neck, and the ring from his hand. "Hear my gesa," the boy said. He let his knife drop into the grass. "By the goddess, I will take neither food nor drink until this woman—" he swallowed—"this woman tells me who I am." He turned from Fedelm and walked from the tuath.

No one touched his things on the hill, though they were marked with the signs of our family. When everyone was gone I saw them still in the long grass, bold as the gold teeth of the old tinker who sold locks of mermaid hair in Kilronan Bay.

Mael Duin went five days without food and water. Fedelm stayed in her house. My mother went to her but she would say nothing. I heard my parents talking late at night; they thought Fedelm had lost her mind. Mael Duin worked on his curragh, stripped bark, slept in the woods and spoke to no one. Then on the fourth day he went out on the lake in his curragh. Germane and I stayed most of that day and the next on the lake, fishing, always keeping Mael Duin in sight but never speaking to him.

On the fifth day Fedelm stood at the edge of the lake for an hour, and at the end of it she called out to Mael Duin. The sun was hot and we were drowsy on the water. Mael Duin rowed in to her, and we drifted into shore, a little distance away. They disappeared in the trees. It was almost night before we found out that he was gone.

I was Diuran Leccerd, anstruth—the half-poet, when Nuca and I went home again. Four years were gone and the ogam strokes on my staff came up to my thigh. I had passed my father's height by a head, and my druid staff stood against the wall of his house. I tried not to inhale the stench of roast venison; it didn't seem to bother

Nuca, although he too ate only bread and cheese. The table had been cleared when Germane, pouring a second cup of hot mead, spoke softly into my ear.

"Mael Duin is here. He's waiting for you."

My father didn't look up; his eyes were fixed on a space beyond his bowl. He nodded at my half-gesture of apology and mumble of thanks for the meal. There would be no argument about Mael Duin tonight.

I used the trick of distancing and the room stretched. My mother lit the oil lamp. It soared, a burnished crescent moon with her horns up, high into the rafters. My father sat below, deep in the room with bent head, his hands warmed by the sides of his bowl. His long fingers made a circle around it; his thumbs were asleep under the curling steam. I have my father's hands.

We took his curragh, Germane steering behind and I in front with the long paddle. It was still and grey on the shore before us. The boat came up on the sand with a hush. I made a fire on the beach while Germane went off into the woods to find Mael Duin. For a long time I stood watching a rain cloud cross the lake. It looked like a shield moving over the water.

There was a noise, and I turned around. Mael Duin stood behind me. He was dressed as a warrior, naked under a cloak with a torc and armrings made of thorns. But he carried no weapons, except a hunting spear. A leather satchel hung from his shoulder by a rope. He was tall and lean, his eyes were fever-bright, and his gold hair was cut close to his skull. When I stood up, he stepped back.

"Are you sick?" I asked, going to him. Germane grabbed my wrist.

Mael Duin crossed to the opposite side of the fire. "I've come to see the druid," he said, his voice hoarse and dark. "I can't come into the tuath. Caideac. Un-clean—I'm contaminated. Will you bring Nuca? I need weapons; I need his help."

He squatted straight down on the ground, taking the skin satchel into both hands, holding it carefully like something wounded. Germane and I sat down across from him. "When I went from the tuath," he said, "I went first to Kildare, the monastery of St. Brigid, where Fedelm said my mother was prioress. They took me to her."

We listened. I didn't know if what Mael Duin had found there had destroyed him, but he was still proud. Some things he told us that night, and some later, at sea. I have dreamt of them myself for many years, since the end of the voyage.

At the south side of the cathedral of St. Brigid, at a small distance from the flame that is never extinguished, the ground opens up, and a ladder descends into a small, dark cave.

When Mael Duin climbs down, he finds a woman, alone, covered in a filthy blanket. She twists a bit of wool around a stick, looking up at him, then dropping her eyes as if she can't make up her mind about something. Then, still looking at the stick in her hands and smiling, she says: "I had a beautiful house in the lake. You never saw a more perfect domed roof, smooth-thatched. At night we watched the moon appear in the chimney hole, a lamp above our bed. It made shadows on my husband's face the way I loved him."

She stops and looks into Mael Duin's face. After a moment she grabs his arm, pinching it, and asks him, "Did you know him?" He shakes his head and she lets go. "His name was Ailill at the Edge of Battle; he said it to me; chieftain of a tribe of the Eoganacht, a lord of the king of Cashel. He gave me a brooch of gold with apples in silver; he gave me silks I wove with gold thread for our bed; he gave me cattle and pigs and a red heifer for my own. He gave me a child, but I gave it away."

She closes her eyes and puts one hand on her forehead, and then lets it slide to her cheek, as if to feel for a fever. "No one had a more beautiful house than I." She gasps and her eyes open wide. "I saw the roof twigs floating smashed on the water. I saw his head come back torn off at the neck, dirt around his mouth, his eyes shut.

"In my dreams the Vikings always come quietly," she says slowly, explaining. "You understand. A knife cutting butter. They come from the sea, across the lake, up the river. He rode to Dooclone Church. Sanctuary." She shakes her head, scolding. "I told him to be careful, but he wouldn't listen. He kissed me there, up there, by the door. I was unlucky, and he was dead. Fedelm took the baby for her own. Nobody knew.

"No one is safe," she whispers, coming very close to him, "from the goddess. Be careful. She has three faces." She holds out three fingers. "When her hair is gold, her mouth red as rowanberries, she takes lovers. I had one." She touches Mael Duin's sleeve with one finger, then curls it into her fist. "I had one, his hair thick as a wolf's collar, but soft as silk. He gave me a brooch of silver apples when I wore her second face, when I felt life stirring inside. It's lost. I couldn't find it." She clutches his arm. "The Vikings took it," she says, then turns away from him, and crosses the dirt floor.

"Sometimes when I'm walking under the moon I feel her breath on my neck, on my bald head. She falls in step behind me, and we walk together, whispering about this and that. She shows me places under rocks and behind trees where blood still seeps. We laugh. Old women are respected for their wisdom." She stops, facing him, the smile trailing from her mouth. "Who are you?"

"I am Mael Duin," he answers.

"Mael Duin. That was it. Mael Duin. The shorn-haired man. I was so foolish—I named him Mael Duin. If I had a son I would make him take heads, but I have nothing for my third face but shame. I shouldn't have lost that brooch with the silver apples. It was unlucky." She pulls the blanket up over her face. Mael Duin touches her shoulder, then the cropped gold head, and she lowers the blanket. "You're a pretty boy," she says, and begins to cry. "Go away."

"Please. Can you tell me about him, about Ailill Ocar Aga?"

"Him? I only met him once. Up there, by the chapel door. It was dark." She laughs. "You can see that place—sunk in—by the step, where he knelt. Him? He never said a prayer."

Then Mael Duin leaves his mother and goes into the valley of the great forest of oak trees where the king of the Eoganacht has lived with his lords for a thousand years or more. There lies Cashel, the dark stone fort that floats above the oak trees, against the luminous fog that fills the valley. I have seen a silver spear of light beneath the cloud, beginning at the right wall of the fortress and circling the whole horizon until it finished at the left wall. But no one knows where the raw stone ends and the cut stone of the rising wall begins.

It's night, and somewhere above a dog barks, and another, and the king's hounds appear, silver wolf-hounds, taller than a man when they stand up. A door opens in the small cottage at the foot of the rock. A boy looks out and closes the door again. A moment later a man comes out, with a spear point flashing in the lamplight beside his face.

"Who are you?" he asks the young stranger at his door.

"A traveler. Mael Duin, of the Eoganacht."

"The Eoganacht? Your speech is strange."

"I have lived in the west, in Connaught."

"What do you want?" he asks.

"I'm looking for Ailill Ocar Aga, the king's man."

The man looks into Mael Duin's face, and behind him, into the fog. After a moment he says, in an odd way, with a bit of a smile, as if he were answering a riddle or seeing the end of a joke at his own expense, "Ailill Ocar Aga is dead."

"Are you his kin?"

"He has no kin. He's been dead these fifteen years. You can have no claim on him—I said he has no kin alive to pay a debt of blood or gold, if that's your business."

"Did you know him, then?"

"I knew him. What do you want? Who are you?"

"His son. Do I have the look of him?"

"Are you crazy? He had no son." The boy looks at him and begins to turn away. "No, wait!" The man holds the lamp up higher. "Come closer to the light. You have no mark of the Eoganacht on you—can you show me something with the name on it?" Mael Duin shakes his head. "How old are you?"

"Sixteen," answers Mael Duin.

"Sixteen. Your voice is deep for a boy. Well, come inside, by the fire. The fog is coming in close. There's no one will talk to you tonight above; the Rock is shut up tight." Mael Duin follows him into the cottage. There is a turf fire burning in the hearth, and a drowsy, dark-eyed cow hanging her head over the low wall that divides the room. The man drags a mattress stuffed with heather in front of the hearth and motions to Mael Duin to sit down. He hooks the lantern into the pitch-blackened ceiling of thatch, pours out a glass of ale into a shallow blue cup, and puts it down by Mael Duin's hand.

"My friend Ailill never stepped out of bed without spear and dagger. You have no weapons about you. Who told you that you were his son?"

"A woman. From Kildare."

"He did go to the mountains above Kildare before he died, raiding with the king. Maybe fifteen, sixteen years ago now."

"How did he die?"

The man says slowly, "In a raid."

The door opens and a dark-haired young man comes in with an armful of turf that he stacks by the hearth.

"This is my son, Brian. He's seventeen this day. Ailill at the Edge of Battle was to be his own foster father, and train him in the arts of war, but then he died when Brian was only a boy."

Brian says, "I remember him, though. Sitting here, by the fire. He was tall—"

"So he was—that's no illusion, though you were only a child—"

"And his eyes were dark, like lapis, his hair black, and his face—to me he had an eagle's face. I was afraid of him; he was so quiet, but he moved quickly; he took me into his lap and we watched the fire."

"He was chief of his own tribe in the southwest," says his father, and turning to Mael Duin, "I don't know what's left of it, but maybe there would be some people glad to welcome you. I'll send you on there tomorrow, when the fog lifts."

So Mael Duin found the tribe of Ailill Ocar Aga, by the sea, and the people of the tuath took him in, the son of their chief. I know what he was to the Eoganacht, how he won all their games by his skill and his luck, how the young boys followed him around from dawn until night. For three years he was a hero to them, son of their dead hero. But then, one day in early spring, the goddess turned against him and he saw the truth.

Mael Duin is pitching stones over the burnt rafters of a ruined church. Dooclone it is called, by the sea. Brian of Cashel, who became his friend, and the boys of the Eoganacht are watching him. Briccne, the crippled care-taker of Dooclone Church, also stands and watches. Mael Duin throws a stone over the church and it clears the center arch. He walks into the ash, looking for a flat stone, puts his hand on a huge skull, and draws it out. He steps back to get clear, to take aim, and Briccne takes hold of his shirt, mumbling nonsense. The boys laugh.

"It would be better to avenge the man who was killed here than to throw stones over his bare, burnt bones," hisses Briccne.

"What are you talking about? Whose bones?" Mael Duin asks. He looks down at his hand, and he sees a big black ant come out of the eyehole, then cross his thumb.

"There's none here, but your own father's, the hero Ailill at the Edge of Battle, who ran here to hide and was killed by Vikings. He grew mouldy here under the rafters with no one coming forward to defend or to bury him. The Vikings burned Dooclone over his head." Briccne stops and wipes his mouth. "Have you not listened to the old men talk in their drink? Ask them sometime about the Vikings. They'll tell you the plans they have for wrecking them on the coast, if the fog is right; but it never is. Ask them about Ailill Ocar Aga and they'll tell you he was a hero. If you say one word about what I've told you here they'll shut their doors in your face.

"You can hear the truth of it yourself if you don't believe me. In the harbor at an Daingin the same Vikings come summers for poteen; they have a tower on an island beyond. I've heard them myself bragging that no one had the guts to stand for Ailill Ocar Aga, or to avenge his death. But you're smart to stay away; you have his face."

Mael Duin left the Eoganacht. He made a skin sack for his father's skull, and cut his hair off, and walked alone north and west to Lough Corrib, looking for the druid Nuca.

There, in the low firelight, it was not hard to see his father in him, the man at the edge of battle. There was a tension in him, something coming off his skin, and especially from his dark eyes. It was like a pressure or a sound—like an ax blade sharpened, just out of hearing.

"Diuran, can you tell where a boat is going by the feel of the sea? By a warm current or a cold, or by the kind of bark that appears, or how a log spins between the waves? Do you know all the stars that rise out of the western sea?"

I answered him, "I know these things by heart from the fishermen of Aran, but Mael Duin, I have never killed a man. What are you going to do?"

"Find them."

The wind was light and warm; I could hear waves lapping on the stones. " 'When the sea covers the three Aran Islands behind you, then keep the North Star above the bow. Five days out clear sailing and let the gannets fly. Follow the birds and cover the mast with Viking skulls.' "

"Navigator?" Mael Duin asked. It was dark, and I couldn't see his face, but I felt the hair standing up on my arms.

"I will," I said.

"And helmsman," said Germane, as he put a branch on the dying fire.

We didn't talk for awhile. Fedelm's wolfhound came up and lay with its head on Mael Duin's lap. She lifted her head when he moved his hand to take a torch from Germane and set it into the sand. I saw the flame shake above his hand, then stand straight up as he let go and pulled the skin sack in closer to him. I slept on the beach, and that night, in my dreams, I heard distant thunder and the sound of a new blade hammered.

The next morning I took Nuca across the lake and left him at the shore. Mael Duin was somewhere up in the trees above the steep hillside. I climbed to the top and sat on the wall beside the stile, looking down at the green pasture—our grazing land for four hundred years and more, crossed again and again by stone fences that traced the profile of the land, following each rise, dip, and curve in the hillside—and the silver ponds reflecting the clouds like glass. The clouds moved together, slowly, like cattle across the sky. There were silver lines of light on the lake below, moving too, slowly up to the edge of the fog. Beyond the small grey island, at the far side of the lake, the crannogs were rooted in cloud. The cloud grew brighter as I watched, and somewhere a lamb cried. Then Mael Duin was coming down the hillside.

At first I thought Nuca had gone, but then I saw that he was still standing by the curragh with his face to the lake. There was nothing about him that caught the light; his clothes were the color and texture of bark, moss and stone. It was something I had grown used to, but knowing Mael Duin would reach him first at the shore made me look again. The druid had a way of standing quieter than any animal I'd ever tracked and lost, seeing too late. He turned and thrust his staff into the sand, his hand on the top, round and smooth as the joint of a leg bone. I came down behind Mael Duin and stopped.

Nuca said nothing at first; he stood between Mael Duin and the lake, looking at him and twisting the knob of his staff in his hand. Mael Duin didn't move; his eyes were closed, or nearly so from the glare of the lake, and his breath was coming slow; I could see the mist.

There was a shriek; the lake wobbled, and went dark. Nuca stood with his mouth open, laughing. He stopped abruptly and peered at Mael Duin, who stood rigid. "Diuran," he called me in his own voice, half jackdaw and half whisper, "build a fire there. Not too close to the water." He ran the tip of his staff along a ridge of big stones that were partially crusted with moss. He went to the curragh and came back with a dark grey cloak folded over his arms. "He can wear this and keep his sack with the bone in it. Burn the rest: clothes and weapon. Then don't interrupt, or you'll have to leave us."

First I laid the strange spear with the curved handles of the Eoganacht on the steaming rocks, then his cape, wrapped about lengths of brittle hawthorn. Nuca called Mael Duin to the fire.

"Weak minds follow laughter with laughter," Nuca growled, prodding the smoking turf with his staff. "I could do nothing for you, then. You stood back; but it's a simple test, and shows little." He stirred the fire. "You wear your hair like Cuchulain, the hero who sought his own death. That is also the way we have of marking a lunatic—shaving his head. Only the goddess knows what

70

a man can do when he is opened. There are certain powers, and you have always been lucky.

"You would do this alone. Carrying a sword in one hand and your father's skull in the other. But believe me, boy who has walked on the bones of his father, you need the protection of the goddess whom you have also betrayed. She has given you gifts, and you have given nothing back. Yes, you've joined the tuath at her festival, but you have never acknowledged her. In this mission she will join you. She will send you dreams, and waking visions that you will perhaps not survive. And if you go unafraid to this ordeal, you may see the white ash in the keel of your boat curl and snap and all your crew drown, or your own sword turning in your flesh. It won't matter if you believe or not if she is against you."

Mael Duin knelt and stretched his arms towards the fire. "But the Vikings are only men; any animal can be tracked and killed, if the hunter doesn't give up. I won't give up. I'm not afraid of death."

"No, you're not; you welcome it. But you don't see the danger." Nuca touched the satchel with his hand, and Mael Duin flinched. "There's another way. She'll take you back if you kill yourself now. You could make an offering. Here is my knife. No one will stop you. We'll carry the body of the boy Mael Duin back to the tuath and who will blame you? Everyone would understand; it is better to be dead than outcast. It's the easiest way, easiest for someone like you."

I thought I should speak, to make Nuca stop. Mael Duin's pride would never let him turn back from a challenge of cowardice. Mael Duin sat with his hands clenched on his knees. Nuca watched him. Then he said, "Believe me, she will take you in the end, one way or the other."

Mael Duin looked up. "I'm not going to kill myself; I won't fail, Nuca. The Vikings don't dream of a son, a son of the warrior Ailill Ocar Aga. It's they who don't see the danger." He spoke slowly, whittling down the image of his thought to something small and sharp. "They'll come back. Like the redwing thrush. After every harvest they come, from the north, to Erin—to an island off Slea Head in an Daingin. To feed on our land. They have built a tower on the bones of an Irish ringfort; they hang their walls with the gold shields and torcs and armrings of the Eoganacht. But their safety is a lie. When they dream, I will be coming. When they wake and think of me, my sword will come down on their necks."

He paused. "I'm not afraid, Nuca."

"That is unfortunate. Well." He closed his eyes for a moment. "When you make your gesa, when you swear your oath to avenge his death, the whole tuath will take you in. If you succeed they'll forget everything; they'll make the outcast chieftain. And my boy will never become a druid. Be quiet, Diuran; did you think I would forbid it?" He looked back at Mael Duin. "The summer days are long, but you have much to learn. I wonder if they are long enough for you?"

"I'll do whatever you say."

"Yes; you'll follow every direction in detail. Maybe, at least, you can learn caution." He stood up.

"Thank you, Nuca." Mael Duin stood up and put the sack rope over his shoulder. "I have asked Diuran to come, as navigator."

Nuca nodded, and knocked the head off a scarlet mushroom with the end of his staff.

Mael Duin went on. "I need an oceangoing curragh. The Vikings go north again at Samhain. I have three months."

"First you will pass a rite of purification, a sacrifice here at the meeting stone, and then I will consult the spiral stones above Poulnabrone for the correct time of setting out. We'll need the bone for that. It is the eve of Beltane, the cross-quarter day, and if we have luck—a clear sky—we may learn something. Then a time of meditation and penance must pass. We'll need forty ox hides for the curragh's skin, soaked in oak bark, or the boat will rot and burst in the sea. Oak for the gunnels and a young ash for the mast. The wood on the north side of the tree is always best. A thousand lengths of hide to knot about the wicker frame, and a hundred birch roots, each strand as long as your leg, to wrap the gunnels. Hide for sails and flax for rope. Then no hand but yours will touch the boat until it's made. And from then until the day the curragh is finished you will speak to no one. There is a place you can stay by the monastery at Cong, an old fish house on the river. You will sleep there when we return from Poulnabrone. The Christians will leave you alone, but you must be careful not to show yourself to any man of the tuath. Take your water from the river, but don't touch the lake. Remember, your mouth, your hands, your body—even your words—are pollution until you make your gesa. While you are building the curragh eat nothing but hazelnuts, salmon and mulberries."

"But the berries are poison—" I said out loud.

"No one has ever died from a bad dream," Nuca answered.

"I need weapons," said Mael Duin.

Nuca reached down into the fire and took out Mael Duin's spear with his hand. He put it under the lake water and held it there for a few moments, then gave it to Mael Duin. "Weapons. Yes. Let's see your famous aim.

73

Why not? Diuran says you've never lost a match. That ash tree, with the broken limb halfway down. Can you hit that? I've seen children make their mark from here."

Mael Duin slowly turned the length of iron in his hand, stepped back and let it fly. He missed. Three times, as we stood watching, the spear went into the grass.

"I could give you the power to hit whatever you aim at, right now. I'm afraid it would cost you a great deal. Would that satisfy you?"

"I used to have that for nothing," said Mael Duin.

"And that's what it was worth."

"The spear is deceptive; it looks straight but falls wide. Does it matter? I'll have another. They say a druid can only make true weapons. When can we begin?"

"By Morrigan who taught us war, the only weapons you will have to kill your father's murderer are those you take from him yourself."

Mael Duin started to walk away.

"Wait," the druid commanded. "Where are you going?"

He stopped. "To an Daingin."

"How will you find it? How will you hold a spear when you can't even stop your hands shaking?

"Nuca, I've never killed a man. You know all the ways. If you will teach me I'll do whatever you say."

Nuca leaned on his staff and stood up. "Diuran, put the spear on the fire. The light is growing. Everyone will be awake soon. Now, son of Ailill Ocar Aga, we begin."

There's a big stone below Rath Cetach in a clearing. No trees grow there, or ever have, just gorse and a kind of heather. We used to play a pebble game out there as boys, because the rock was flat and smooth, and the pebble could roll across and drop into all the different crevices and we could keep score. We never told our parents, or even intended to go there, but somehow we'd end up there.

Rath Cetach was purple and solemn and the rock still had the grey sheen of morning when we began the simple rite of purification. Mael Duin knelt in the bristling heather, his skin bare and rough with cold. I stood beside him with a tethered calf.

Nuca spoke the names of the goddess as he held the skull above the stone.

"Ailill Ocar Aga stands shamed between life and life, and calls his son to avenge him. There is no answer. This son has come to manhood with a false pride. He has desecrated his father's death place. For these crimes it is right that he should die. He is an abomination. Because of his ignorance, and his good intentions, I now ask reprieve. Let him live until he can make amends. He asks nothing of the tuatha or of you until that time. In Mael Duin's place I send this good calf."

Then I brought the animal to him and he made the sacrifice. The calf took the knife without balking, and its blood spread over the stone, filling the chiseled tributaries and lakes in its surface. Nuca gave the skull of Ailill Ocar Aga back to Mael Duin. I put the long cloak over Mael Duin's shoulders. Behind the mountain the sun appeared, and a thrush sang out. The air was soft and cool with a breeze that lifted the long fur on the fallen calf's shoulders. Nuca finished up at the rock. "Now we go south, to Poulnabrone."

The stone was marked by a thin streak of blue smoke when we left the lake and the receding mountain and rode south. Mael Duin told Nuca everything he had told Germane and me the previous night. Nuca was very interested in the description of Ailill Ocar Aga, and he made Mael Duin repeat what Brian had told him several times. Mael Duin said that Brian would come to an Daingin. Then we talked about the curragh, and where to set off for the island, and what we would need for the crossing: turf and a cauldron for cooking, sheepskins for sleeping, cheese, oatmeal and dried meat, and fresh water to drink. It started to rain as we came along the edge of the bay, and then we rode in silence. We turned inland again at the burren, with the rain masking the last glimpses of sea.

The twilight was long on the burren. I could see far in every direction. Although shapes off in the distance seemed to change, what passed under our feet was always the same: black, stunted heather, rough stones and bare turf, some places laid open like deep graves. Then the land seemed completely flat, and there was nothing on the horizon but a frail sheet of rain.

Just as Nuca said, "It's clearing up," suddenly there stood Poulnabrone, the great dolmen, bleak and shining against a clear sky. He was anxious and wanted to hurry, but our horses had to step carefully around the stones. Soon they could go no farther, and we left them. We walked, taking the wet stones one by one, crossing the bog. The stones grew larger as we approached the dolmen.

The old table is made of two upright flagstones, thicker than the door of a cottage and three times the height of a man, with the great capstone lying across them. Where I stood, looking out at the limestone, rough waves frozen on the burren, everything seemed very distant. I had the impression that I was standing in a high place, that the land—even the huge dolmen—dropped away below me on every side. But when I walked up close to the dolmen, I saw that the land it stood on was the higher ground and that the dead who had lain face up on the capstone would be the highest thing of all.

Nuca and Mael Duin were talking. The sky was clear and the moon was rising between the legs of the table. Mael Duin gave him the skin sack, and we followed him behind the dolmen. Nuca stopped before a narrow opening in the ground bridged by stone. "I'll go first," he said. "Follow quickly; we don't have much time."

The passageway was dark and narrow, lined with huge stones, and in several places I had to jam my shoulder through. Mael Duin came after me, cursing softly, and Nuca kept calling back, "Hurry! Hurry!" Then suddenly the passage opened up and at the same time I saw my own shadow across the floor. Nuca pulled my arm, crying out, "Get out of the way, Diuran, it's coming in!" Mael Duin and I stepped back and a beam of light came straight down the passageway, across the floor, and stopped at the bottom of a large stone basin. There was a high corbeled stone ceiling above, and three small chambers coming off the larger central chamber where we stood. The stones lining the chambers were deeply engraved with crescents, spirals and diamonds. The huge basin was in the farthest recess. Nuca knelt beside the edge of the shaft of moonlight.

In the east, when the dragon boats came down the narrow Boyne, the Blackwater, and the Liffey, the people of Meath would move into the old passage graves under the hills. They cooked in the basins and spilled corn for their animals across the chamber floors. As the equal length of day and night drew close they began to see strange lights within the graves. At dawn, out of total darkness, the floor of the chamber would glow like molten copper, as if the great stones were on fire, and then suddenly go dark again. Sometimes there were pale, vaporous lights that moved like cool fingers across the passage walls. They saw images of fire and spinning water in the stones, but the chambers were dry and the people afraid to pasture their animals in the open, or even to let them drink from the river, in case it was poisoned.

The druid Nuca was one who could read the stones. When the moonbeam had passed over the basin and started to move up the wall, Nuca put his hands on the stone. He measured by the width of two fingers the space between the beam and the spokes of a carved wheel. When the light stopped, finally, at the edge of a crescent, and grew stronger, he stood up and looked along the beam towards the outside; then he touched all the places on the standing stones along the passage where the beam lay.

As he came back, the chamber was growing dim again, and he spoke to Mael Duin. "Your luck follows you, Mael Duin. I didn't expect a clear sky. The goddess touches stone with her own finger, showing you the way to your enemy. It is more than you deserve; be grateful. Listen carefully. When the hunter and the dragon are in conjunction, you begin the journey. That day is seventy-one days from this. You will choose sixteen men to go with you; not one more or less. Now, here it is. This night the spirit of Ailill Ocar Aga can be wakened. The moon has come down into the earth, and made an opening to heaven. I must ask him questions. You may hear something through the steam. Listen, but don't speak."

He told me to bring water from the spring beyond the dolmen, for the large basin. Then I was to build a fire, and heat five round stones until they were burning hot, and bring them back inside the chamber. By torchlight I filled the basin with brackish water and set the burning stones under the water. The water started to boil and the chamber filled with steam. I saw Mael Duin give the skin sack to Nuca, and then both crouched down by the basin. Through the dense, spiraling steam Nuca turned blindly towards me and yelled, "Get out!"

I sat outside, leaning against the portal stone, and watched the moon come up over the roof of the dolmen. The horses bent their necks over the gorse and murmured. I took a drink from the spring and spat it out. It tasted of sulphur.

When Nuca and Mael Duin came out of the grave, they were blind and drenched with sweat. Nuca grabbed my arm and whispered, "Don't talk." I led them, both trembling hard, to a shelter of gorse and stone, and covered them with cloaks.

Some time before dawn Nuca woke me, and took me a distance away from Mael Duin. He said, "In a little while we'll ride back. Mael Duin will stay in the monk's fish house, below the chapel at Cong. He will build the curragh. You can bring him what he needs for the boat, but don't speak to him. Now, I'll tell you what you must know as navigator. The falcon-spirit of Ailill took me over the sea to the house of his murderers." Nuca told me which stars were above him, how bright, and how high over the sea. He spoke of the currents below, the color of the waves in darkness and in daylight, and the kinds of fish that flashed in air, and those that streaked like shadows under the waves. He described the rocks of the island, and the sound of the waves going against them.

Then Mael Duin woke, and we rode north, I ahead and Nuca and Mael Duin behind. I looked back into Mael Duin's eyes, focused on distance. There was a slight change, as if something had been simplified, but the same anger burned there. I could feel it in the back of my neck, in my wrists and in the bend of my knees. I saw his anger spread to the bracken on the burren floor where it caught fire, and the flames licked up around our horses' legs, and smoldered at the big rocks on every side. Then the sky over us caught fire, first in a wide stream, and then spreading in ripples like a copper lake, burning. And the sun came up over the burren.

Nobody died that summer. Still, there was a feast and a bonfire every night on the lake. Most nights we sat by the fire, drinking and arguing about boat handling, navigation and Vikings. We talked about weapons and killing thrusts, and kept the bonfire going late. Our parents complained of our foolishness, but it wasn't our fault that we were inexperienced. Our territory had been peaceful, and few of us had had the honor of taking heads. Everyone wanted a private consultation with Nuca, when he could be found, over the selection of weapon runes. There were many marriages recorded and more losses of virginity. When I disappeared from the tuath with a girl for a week Nuca said nothing about it. Once Mael Duin had begun to build the curragh there was little for me to do but watch or get in the way.

She was a quiet girl, and we had a peaceful time drifting and fishing on Loughrea, sleeping on the sand or under the small curragh when it rained. She had a green and violet shawl that I used for a pillow. I can't remember what her voice sounded like, but I can hear the sound of the falls where we stood one morning, and the feel of her fingers laced in my own. I thought of her a lot in the time that followed.

The tuath thought of nothing but magic and omens.

The mothers of the chosen crew were secretive and short-tempered; their houses stank of valerian and wild garlic. Germane's shield fell off the wall one evening, and my mother cried all night long, begging my father not to let him go. Clouds were ominously red, then gray, then yellow. Dogs howled and birds screeched at the wrong hours. Old people remembered things long forgotten and objects lost were mysteriously recovered. People remembered their dreams. There was a new terror among the children, that Mael Duin—the ogre with the long arm—might reach down their chimney and snatch them out of bed. If smoke came crooked out of somebody's chimney the girls clutched at each other and screamed. By evening their fright was forgotten and you could see them through the open doors of the crannogs, with fires going behind them, comparing the length of stitches in a piece of leather sail or the dyes in a lover's cloak. Ardan, Cailte and Seamus were angry because Mael Duin had not chosen them to be among his crew; they said he was crazy and the voyage unlucky. But nobody paid much attention to them.

Nuca sent me often to the fish house on the river with loads of leather or flax. It was a small stone house, no more than four or five paces wide in each direction, built out over the water, with the constant sound of the river moving fast beneath. There was a simple hearth, two small arched windows looking out east and west over the river, and a slit in the stone floor for a salmon net or hook. A low arched threshold led to a stone landing and a narrow, slippery footpath to the riverbank. Rowan and willows and beeches spread out from the bank in a canopy over the thatched roof; swans sheltered under the branches when it rained. The berries were ripe, and Mael Duin's hands and face were stained red by midsummer. His hair grew back, and though he was thin from his diet of berries and hazelnuts, he never seemed to sleep, nor was he tired. He worked hard and fast and maintained his silence, only nodding to me when I came or when I stood from my log-bench to go. But there was an easiness between us; I remember the quiet, and always—suspended in the constantly changing light of the woods as he worked and moved around the boat—the fight to come.

No one but Mael Duin could touch the boat while it was made, hidden away in the glade, where bright moss grew thick on the ground and on every inch of bark. There, in a triangle of ground between three birch trees, the bones became flesh. She was huge—the length of twelve men lying head to foot, a great whale skeleton lying belly up in the woods. He fastened the white ash frame with ten thousand leather thongs, cut and soaked by the tuath on the lake. Every knot began and ended with a pass of his right hand over the left, as Nuca had taught him. I brought oak heart for the gunnels. Fern seeds were plentiful and Nuca scraped them from the underside of the fronds; tucked between the overlaps of hide they would help make the boat invisible to enemies, as they make the nesting lake birds disappear along the shore.

While Mael Duin sewed the forty stinking hides together over the curragh's hull with flaxen thread and began to rub wool grease over the thongs and overlaps of hide, I found the young ash tree Nuca required for mast and oars. We cut the mast from the north-facing side for strength and give. The solstice passed, and the days began to shorten. Everyone worked quickly. The leather sails were ready, and the last flaxen ropes were drying in the trees. Mael Duin rubbed pitch into the seams, and the curragh was nearly finished. I was meeting the girl with the green shawl every night, and one afternoon, when I walked into my father's house, she was sitting on a stool by the fire, talking to my mother and winding yarn. After that she ate every meal with us, and when my mother gave me the cloak they'd been weaving she was proud showing me the parts each had done.

When I brought the finished oars to the woods I saw a new scar on Mael Duin's arm, and I knew that the figures cut into the mast were stained with more than rowan-berries. His curragh was going into unfamiliar seas, but with the taste of his father's blood on her, she could follow his murderer blind. One thing remained. When Mael Duin put his curragh into the water for the first time, when he appeared to the tuath and made his oath, a secret change would take place. Something known only to him, Nuca and myself. I was navigator but he would set the course. His soul would be passed into the curragh. I didn't believe that it was more than ritual; still the moment of the gesture was inevitable, and I didn't like to think about it.

Then one afternoon the smith fires were cold and only the little hearth smoke drifted above our lake. The clanging of new iron and bronze had stopped. Children had gone in from their play on the beach at noon and not returned although the day was clear and warm. My mother kept back a lamb for the last noon meal. When Germane and I were getting ready to leave, my father stopped me at the door and gave me a knife he'd had since he was a boy. He put it in my hands and said that maybe if I didn't waste all my time talking poetry I'd be a hard fighter to match.

It was the time of evening when grass and leaves are shot straight through with green fire. Green is always the last color before dark. And will be at the end of life and time. When nothing moves or breathes Erin will be lit with a green fire, until the hills go out. It is the last clarity at every deathbed, a trick of the goddess.

It had come quickly. The boat was finished and the tuath was gathered on the far shore. We were seventeen on our side under the trees, waiting for the druid's signal. Now I watched the color drain from the oak leaves, each tree a mass of open hands. And suddenly it was night. I couldn't distinguish people in the moving crowd any-more, just random, bobbing points of light through the mist. On their side, the tuath, a torch in each hand, also watched and waited. Then in one gesture the mist lifted, the lights froze and we raised the curragh over our heads.

With eight it was easy to carry. At the lake edge we brought it over and down. Nuca said something to Mael Duin, and he nodded. Germane set the flares in a row deep into the sand, then we slipped the boat into the black water and took up oars. Now they could see us coming on the far side, with light behind us. A child laughed and dropped his torch; two lights separated from the crowd of lights and moved off. Above the slosh of oars Nuca spoke a prayer and poured phosphorescent oil on the water. "Calm seas, safe voyage."

Mael Duin sat in the prow with his back to us, his voice hoarse from disuse and the strange words halting. It was the language of our fathers whom we destroyed by their fear of iron, the Tuatha da Danaan, people of the goddess Danu.

"I have finished my boat, Danu.
Triple hide,
Perfect crescent,
Arc of cattle horn,

Silver headdress for your triple face,
Be swift and steady.
Smell out the killer. He's taken my name, my shield,
   my face.
Let me take his life.
Make his voice loud and careless.
Let him say once more that he killed Ailill Ocar Aga
   and was never challenged.
Keep hidden, Danu.
When he's alone in the dark let him see nothing in it.
Let him look at a rock in sunlight and see its shape
   only. Let him sleep without dreams.
This boat moves, is blood.
The name of the boat is Mael Duin, the soul of man."

I lay awake for a long time that night, thinking about
the time Mael Duin had slept beside me when I was
leaving home for the first time. I was fourteen that year.
Tonight Mael Duin's eyes had kept everyone at a distance, but after all, they said, he'd been with the druid.
Tonight I'd listened with my family to Nuca's poem for
him, knowing it was I that should have been singing
instead of standing there, dreaming by the fire. As the
poem reached its height I saw in every face a longing to
be going, and even in the women that it was a great
thing. Now and then someone moved; metal struck
metal. We were a huddle of weapons—bronze, iron and
gold—shapes carved by firelight. Mael Duin leaned back
from the fire against a big fallen cedar. The children sat
behind him, watching, until finally a little girl crawled
into his lap and fell asleep. He stroked her hair absently,
and then the others came closer until there wasn't a bit of
him left to lean against or touch.

And Nuca sang his ending in that voice like an old

squirrel scolding. It wasn't a bad voice, but the pleasure it gave was the pleasure of being scratched, not stroked. Still the words were smooth and even, and they worked on us like a riptide in a quiet bay, a sudden current that pulls you down. Nuca said:

"This boat moves, is blood.
He breathes and the boat moves forward.
This is the grace of Mael Duin."

The people replied:

"This is the grace of Mael Duin."

"He waits for the death thrust
With no weapons beside him.
This is the grace of Mael Duin."

"This is the grace of Mael Duin."

"He tastes iron and the spear
Snaps in midflight.
This is the power of Mael Duin."

"This is the power of Mael Duin."

"The blade returns to its maker
Breaking his heart with a thrust.
This is the power of Mael Duin."

"This is the power of Mael Duin."

"He sleeps beside his father in the West
A Viking skull grins between them.
This is the pride of Mael Duin."

"This is the pride of Mael Duin."

"Till black sheep turn white
Till ogam and stone be blended together
Shall his name be spoken."

"Shall his name be spoken."

"Immram Curaig Mael Duin
The name of the boat is the name he seeks
The name of the boat is the name he saves
The name of the boat is judgment."

THE VIKINGS

3

I opened my eyes and saw the chimney hole still black above me. Dust rotated, suspended in the aura of my mother's lamp. I had watched the specks of gold rise and fall when I was a child, sick and made to stay in bed, at night when the adults were talking late at the table because the cows were dying and no medicine or words would stop it. Now I could hear Germane and my father talking outside. My mother was moving around the room, folding blankets and setting them by the door next to packages of dried meat, oatcakes, and jars of ale.

I strapped the long knife to my thigh and waited by the gate of the woven wall that circled the crannog. Soon the half-empty curragh took us on and we rowed from crannog to crannog, gathering men, food and weapons. We drifted slowly past the black furred remains of the bonfire, past Fedelm's house with its shroud of blue smoke at the head of the lake, past the trail that led up to Rath Cetach. There was hardly a ripple on the lake, not even a dragonfly. The crannogs floated like hay mounds in a pasture of clouds.

Then we drifted along the shore, where the family was now gathered, and Nuca, wrapped in a brown cloak, nodding, with his eyes fixed on the distance, and last, a little apart from the rest, the child who'd slept in Mael Duin's cloak. She had a white goat on a leash, and stood solemn and straightbacked, with her yellow curls tied back in a dark scarf.

Eleven days we rowed and carried the curragh, from river to river, with some portages of half a day between water. But the fair weather of high summer held, and the farther south we traveled the warmer the sun. We caught the great Shannon and rode her down to the mouth, taking turns at the steering oar, giving our backs a rest those two days. Luck stayed with us, and the crossing was calm. By the time we reached the peninsula, an Daingin, all the stiffness and soreness had worn off, and we rowed together with ease.

We camped our first night in the mountains above Gleann na nGealt, the valley of the mad. Nuca had told me about the valley where madmen came even from Gaul and Rome to drink water from the creek and eat the watercress that grew there and be cured of their mental sickness, but we had never gone so far south in our walks over the west of Erin. The valley was shaped like a steep-sided bowl, with a wedge cut out on the sea. The hillsides were treeless. There was a bright twilight when Germane and I walked down the smooth path to the bottom. As we came close to the stream, hidden by low flanks of hazel and alder, I looked up along the rim of the valley. No one could enter without being seen at a great distance, and there was always escape through the opening on the sea. Gleann na nGealt was a safe place. Germane disappeared into the brush and I followed him in. Water poured over the rocks and through the deep ferns and waist-high cress, still green although the hour approached midnight. We said that we would come back when everything was over.

Nuca had given us fourteen days to reach the end of the peninsula, Slea Head, that faced the Blasket Islands and the Viking islands, invisible, beyond. So we had three days camping on the steep cliffs above the cove. The shallow water was turquoise, and we could see sheep grazing on the nearest island, it was so clear. We talked late each night under bright stars and a mild wind. Mael Duin went over all the facts he had about the Vikings from the Eoganacht, and more that he'd gotten from the fishermen who traded in an Daingin and fished off the islands. Brian told his story of Ailill Ocar Aga. On the second day Ardan, Seamus and Cailte appeared without explanation at our camp. Mael Duin spoke to them easily and wouldn't order them off, so I said nothing. They made themselves useful, polishing bronze, filling our casks with fresh water, and I never heard a bitter word out of them; so their coming, and the reconciliation, seemed another piece of luck for the journey.

The shepherds who lived in the beehive clochans on the hillside stood and watched us all day. At night the fishermen came. The cove was lined with their small black-skinned curraghs, some with small masts for sailing out to the islands, but most with only four pins on the gunnels for oars. They wouldn't touch our boat but they asked questions and shook their heads.

She rose like a huge scythe out of the grass, but you could see the shadow she'd cast running before a wind, only a line on the waves from the mast, like the mark a branch throws down on leaves in the forest floor. The ox hide was stained a purplish black from the oak bark and the grease; at true dusk she disappeared. Her hull was wide and shallow; she drew little water, no more than the span from fingers to elbow. Nuca had warned that because of her size if she turned over we'd never get her righted again, and death would come fast in the freezing sea. But with the wind behind or before she was steady, and Germane could keep us moving straight into a wave, if any man's strength could do that.

There were stars on the morning of departure. I hoped it was clear in Connaught, too, and that somehow Nuca would know that it was another piece of luck, a sign that his plan was working. Mael Duin was tense, and paced along the cliff while the crew lowered the boat with ropes into the cove. I walked to the edge of the grass and stood beside him, looking down. The underside of each wave was the color of salmon. I unbuckled my long knife and refastened it; it was rubbing against my thigh and the place was raw. "Let's go," he said, and started down the cliff, his cloak blowing. I slung my shield over my shoulder, picked up my staff and followed him down.

I took my place behind him in the bow, wrapped my weapons in my cloak and put them under the seat. The boat rocked and creaked in the water. The sun came up, and a gold light vibrated over the sand, the limestone cliffs, and our skin. The mist was breaking off the cliffs; huge pieces of gold wool floated out over the water and vanished. At the top of the cliffs the fishermen watched, and at the end of the point, a ram lifted its head from the grass. Everything was perfectly still. The sea lapped on the rocks. I looked back and saw Brian fixing the leather sack to the mast. The wind twirled it around the pole. The sails were wrapped about the mast; we would row out of the breakers before putting them up. He came back down the boat and hooked his seat with its leather thong onto the gunnel directly behind me. Germane yanked the steering oar out of its frame. I pulled up my oar and dropped the handle over the pin on the left gunnel. In a moment sixteen oars dipped into the sea. The boat slowly swung out and around and faced west. Mael Duin's back straightened, and his oar paused over his head, then down and we were on our way.

There was Brian of Cashel, of the tribe of the Eoganacht, and Mael Duin's kinsman by blood; Diarmaid and Donncha from Achill, sons of Fedelm's brother, and good oarsmen; Paidin, their cousin, who was small and could climb up a rope or a mast without twisting it; and Brendan, with his shaved head, who was a Christian monk from the abbey at Cong by the fish house, and wanted to see the western sea. The rest were from our tuath. Sean was the blacksmith's son and could mend weapons; Seamais and Tomais were quiet but the best fishermen on the lake; Conall, Fergus and Iaeg had lived with foster parents in the east and had been in battle every spring since they were fifteen. Daire was missing three fingers on one hand from a boar's tusk when he was four and his sister left him in the woods while she was kissing a stranger, but he could make a fine stew out of a stringy bird, and handle a knife with his other hand better than anyone else in the tuath. Dubthach and Fiacha were black-haired twins who had tied for first place in the games every year since Mael Duin had left the lake. Germane, Mael Duin and I made seventeen.

We were just coming up on the rocks, backpaddling hard, when there was a splash and a scream. Mael Duin's foster brothers were swimming towards us. They had climbed out along the cliff and waited until we drew near, then jumped into the sea. Mael Duin yelled, "Go back!" but Seamus was treading water beside us, sputtering and laughing, "We'll swim out after you! We're not going back!"

My own legs still ached from walking out into the surf. I knew in the cold sea they would tire quickly. Cailte was swimming back towards Ardan, who was choking. We were moving quickly into the rocks, and the boat was swerving in the churning water. Mael Duin was screaming above the breakers at Cailte and then at Germane, who was shouting that we couldn't go back—we had to move forward or go over. Cailte was trying to swim towards the boat and hold onto Ardan at the same time. A wave broke over him and he let go. Ardan's head went under. Cailte couldn't find him. The curragh jerked and there was a splash and Mael Duin was in the sea.

94

He came up quickly on my side and we pulled Ardan up first. Somehow we got them all into the boat without capsizing. The three brothers fell in a heap under the mast, soaking us, soaking the sheepskin blankets, panting and laughing. Ardan heaved up a lot of water, grinned, and looked around. Cailte shook the water out of his black hair and yelled "Thanks!" to Mael Duin, who wasn't looking at him, but at Germane and then at the rocks before us. And then we were into the breakers.

It was like being trapped in a brawl. There was no way to tell where the next blow would come from. Slammed into a wave, no time to see anything—to get some bearings—I just kept pulling hard. It had to stop, but it didn't stop; it changed.

It got quiet. The boat slowed down. A giant wall of water rose up above us. It was like being in the bottom of a huge cauldron. I couldn't see over the sides. I thought: This is the last thing I'm going to see. Then suddenly we began to climb. At the crest the boat careened like a top as its spin breaks down into a wobble. I was sure we'd go over. But the bottom dropped away and we were back down in the hole. For some reason I started to laugh, and then I felt as though my chest had been caved in. Brian had struck me on the back, thinking I had swallowed a wave and was choking. And back up we went. It was hard to decide which was worse, being up or down. But I began to look forward to going up; if it was a last look I was getting, at least it was a look. At the top I could see the Blasket Islands ahead or behind me as they swerved on the horizon.

And then, without warning, we came out of the swells, and it was incredibly still. Ardan was hunched down, grabbing the mast. Germane, still gripping the handle of the big oar as we drifted farther from the roar,

said, "You can come out now, Ardan, we're home."
Ardan didn't move. Germane held his dripping oar above
Ardan, and that stirred him. It took three of us an hour
to bail the curragh out with the leather buckets, but then
the boat was dry and we passed around a cask of ale to
celebrate. Our hull was perfect, no leaks. Mael Duin
ordered the sails up and Brian raised them. We stowed
the long oars away and flew across the waves with a brisk
westerly wind behind us.

We passed a small curragh without sails rowing for
Slea Head, trailing a mass of shiny flounder. Then there
was nothing at all between us and the Blaskets. The
sheepskins and the blankets were hung up to dry in the
wind on ropes, and everybody worked on his weapons,
unwrapping packages of steel and bronze, drying and
polishing. Somebody told a story they had heard in
Donegal about a Viking who attacked his own family
because he thought he'd been poisoned by a piece of
spoiled fish. The Vikings are constantly afraid of poison,
because if they die that way they go to the grave with
nothing but their boots and capes and turn to dirt. If
they die in battle they go to a banquet hall with all their
gold weapons and armour, and blood-drinking virgins
wait upon them throughout eternity. I knew of a special
poison that worked through the skin, so that if a person
only touched it, in a few days he would die, and nothing
could lessen the agony of the death. Nuca and I had
made it up that summer, and I kept it in a small packet
under my cloak.

Mael Duin leaned back against his seat, facing east,
his arms crossed behind his head. There was a band of
unbleached cloth around his head, and a plain gold torc
that the tuath had given him, around his neck, but he
carried no weapons. He had his long legs stretched out,

and his bare feet stuck out of his cloak with the gold hem. I moved so my back blocked the sun, his face in shadow. He passed me his water flask.

" 'A man who is not afraid of the sea will soon be drowned, for he will be going out on a day he shouldn't. But we are afraid of the sea, and we are only drowned now and again.' "

"Once was enough for me."

"A fisherman named Synge told me that, yesterday," said Mael Duin.

"Did Cailte hear him?"

"Maybe he did. He tried to save Ardan, but he couldn't hold him." Mael Duin closed his eyes, and said nothing else. I looked at the sea; there were whitecaps around us. The mast creaked in the thwarts, and the boat moved in a canter; I could feel it bend and straighten below me as it went forward. I tipped the water skin back and swallowed a jet of cold creek water. Mael Duin said suddenly, with his eyes still closed, "Maybe you should have drunk the water at Gleann na nGealt; I heard you laughing when we were in the swells."

"I was scared."

"Because we are twenty now, in the boat?"

"I don't know."

"It won't matter. Cailte's good with a knife. Or give him your bow—you won't need it. If we have to climb up to the house in the dark, and surprise them, you can only carry half of what you brought." Mael Duin sat up and ran one hand along the taut rope over his head. "We're moving fast. . . .

"I can see him, the Viking murderer, even now feeling sick and weak, looking from his window down onto the sea . . . the cold sea . . . the veins in his arms and legs ache, he shudders with cold . . . he is afraid of the moving water, afraid of the shadows under the waves, afraid of the birds circling, afraid of the dark clouds. He sits at the table. Everything he eats and drinks has a sour taste, and his stomach twists and tightens, afraid it is poison, yes, perhaps it is poison. The shadows under the table are the color of blood and he feels, even now, the blood running out of him. Someone whispers the name of Ailill Ocar Aga, and it is like a ghost walking into the room. He cannot get up from the table, he is so weak." Mael Duin's face was perfectly relaxed. I remember thinking, this is something extraordinary, I'll think about this later, not now, just let it be over quickly, or I might be frightened.

"It's going to be easy. And why shouldn't Cailte take one? He's lost something too; he was my younger brother for fifteen years," he said, and smiled. "I'm going to check the ropes," he said, "and give Germane a break at the helm."

I looked at him and saw his profile, sharp like a hawk's, with his bright gold hair like a helmet arcing his head, and only his eyes dark—the same blue as the ocean around us. Then I thought, it's good that he's powerful; then he has a chance to succeed.

"We should see nothing until we get on the other side of the Great Blasket," I said, "and then when the mountain dips below the waves we look west for the first sign of the Viking's island."

"And the sea is full of islands," he said, and went down to the helm.

The sun was at its height when the rocks of the Lesser Blasket loomed close. We passed the island quickly, with a strong shore breeze bending our sails and ropes trailing behind the boat to slow her down. There was a group of girls with sheepskin capes gathering seaweed off the rocks. They waved and we yelled back, flashing our shields. As we passed the curve of their beach they flew off, leaving the coils of black rope on the rocks. Germane, who had been sharing my seat since Mael Duin had taken the steering oar, said they were probably shy and not used to heroes from the mainland sailing by. Tonight they'd have plenty to tell at their hearth, stories of the whale-sized curragh. Maybe tomorrow they'd be the first to tell the story of Mael Duin's curragh and the column of Viking heads on the mast.

Just before the sun went down we saw the Viking island, a faint shape on the horizon. We dropped sail and drifted, waiting for moonrise. Then Mael Duin ordered us to row. The cliffs and a tower became distinct as we drew nearer, and then suddenly we could see the mast of their long ship sticking up behind the tower, and a light appeared in the tower window. Mael Duin turned around, grinning, and whispered, "Follow the light!" He had decided to go in straight under the tower. It was a small island and the ship on the western side would certainly be guarded. An empty strip of sand shined below the tower. With the window as a beacon to guide us, we could take the curragh right up onto the sand.

Mael Duin knelt at the prow, gripping the gunnels. There was no sound but the slap of waves against the hull, a slow drum to call for battle. We drew closer. Our shadows were sharp on the sea, it was so still. There was a man sitting in the east window; he sat on the sill with his back to us. All he had to do was turn around. Oars dipped, pulled and came out; the curragh moved in a trance.

We crossed the tunnel of light that fell from the window. I saw the black bow, the gold of Mael Duin's hair, ropes, oars, bronze and steel weapons pass into the light and out again, then only a patch of murky light on the sea behind us. The man in the window didn't move.

Then we heard laughter and the sound of tables being dragged across stone. The man in the window was pulled away. I heard the Viking language, slurred and coarse. A man with a red beard moved into the window. He caught the top of the window with his hand and leaned back, laughing. He spoke and I clearly heard the name, Ailill Ocar Aga.

I touched Mael Duin's shoulder.

"I see him. He is already dead." We were almost under the tower now, coming in with the tide straight on Germane's oar. "What's the depth, Germane?" Mael Duin called past me.

"Half an oar," he answered.

"Get ready to take her up on the sand. Give me the sack, Diuran," Mael Duin said softly. I untied the sack from its perch on the mast and gave it to him. He wore only a thick weapon belt and leather loincloth. He hooked the skin sack and a plain bronze shield over one shoulder. I strapped my long knife onto my thigh. The boat gave a shudder, and I got ready to jump out. Then a sudden darkness swallowed us.

There was thunder and the curragh began to move like a cradle rocked by a lunatic. Mael Duin screamed out, "No, no, no!" and the storm broke over us.

It must have come from the east, from behind us. I could have sworn the sky was clear before the sun went down. It seemed there were stars, but perhaps not. I remember the moon, hard and cold like a dead eye. She kept peering through the clouds while the storm went on and on. I believed then that she meant to kill us.

We worked all night to save our lives. Three times a

wave broke over the mast. We couldn't bail fast enough. I never believed she could stay upright with so much water in her. Wedged against the oar handle, my iron amulet cut its shape into my hand that night. I lost it near morning, but its mark is still clear in my hand.

THE ROOKERY AND THE ANTS

4

When light came it was quiet, and we were surrounded by fog. The mast was cracked at the thwart. The curragh pitched as each wave went under her, one gunnel high above the other, and the steering oar loose in its frame.

Mael Duin told us to sleep if we could, but keep our weapons close. The Vikings would have to move carefully in the fog, but there was no doubt that they had seen us. If we could repair the mast before they found us, we had a chance. We had to move without a sound. He wrapped the base in rope and pulled, and the mast began to rise slowly, creaking. The curragh evened out, and Germane and I tied off the shrouds. Then we lay down, and Mael Duin started on the ropes. He didn't seem tired at all. I remember when we were boys, repairing a fence. He placed a stone we'd left for last to carry between two or three of us. He wasn't showing off: he'd just come from fishing and it was the only stone left. A few people stood and stared, but no one said a word.

I tried to sleep, but the aching in my muscles was too great. The Viking ship was huge, so with luck we'd see them first. I watched the cloud, looking for a break, a thinning out, a blurred form suddenly taking an edge. It might not be anything at first but a darker place in the fog, easy to miss or ignore. But there was nothing—not a bird or a fish, not even a deadhead or a piece of kelp. The fog muted sound, and I couldn't hear the breakers. I watched one wave as it traveled by me and past the stern, then caught the next at the prow and followed it back. I saw that the water didn't go anywhere, but only changed its shape in place. Then I must have fallen asleep.

When I woke up, the curragh was rocking. It was

darker, and there was a wind. The fog was breaking up. I grabbed my sword.

The clouds above were high and dark, like polished iron. The sky had become what the Vikings call it—the helmet of the wind. Mael Duin stood at the mast, gripping the beam, Germane at the tiller. The rest of us had oars and weapons ready. Which side would the longship appear on? We stared and stared, and then, all at once, the fog simply dissolved. There was nothing there. We looked at the sun going down; there was a path from the horizon across the sea that ended, chipped and broken, in the waves that lapped the hull. We put down our oars and our weapons and then we began to argue.

How far had we drifted in one night and one day? Germane said it didn't matter, that we couldn't sail with the mast cracked, not into any wind. Brian said that it was too dark to decide. In the morning we'd have greater visibility. I said we could start rowing east, and row all night, keeping the wind on our left. We could find a cove on the Blaskets and replace the mast. If we had enough water left. Daire counted nine jars.

"Nine. Only nine," said Mael Duin. He picked up an oar at his feet and ran his hand slowly along the stem. His mouth was hard. No one spoke. The sun was gone and the grey dome of the sky came down on us. The blade grinding started again, more like a pressure than a sound. It was coming off the water, off his skin and from his eyes. There was a crack, and the oar in his hands came apart like a rotten branch.

He looked up at the Viking sky. He said, "In one week or two they'll pack up their boat and go north." He tipped the two pieces of oar off the gunnel. They crossed in the water and floated away, until a wave picked them up and they separated. "They will sail a thousand miles north to their home, but we are lost off the coast of our own land, like a little fishing curragh."

"We can always row east, tomorrow, into the sun," I said. "We'll come up on the coast somewhere—Clare, or an Daingin, or maybe the Arans—"

"You won't go back empty-handed, I swear it. Not one of you," said Mael Duin. "Sleep now. We drift for to-night." Then he went down to the prow.

The wind was light and the curragh drifted. We could have been moving in any direction at all. No stars or moon came out. Mael Duin lay with his left hand in a fist pressed against the hull. There were faint lights in his hair, like the phosphorescence that comes to shore at odd times. Later, when I looked back, he had his head down and his arms stretched out in front of him. There was an eye carved into the hull, below the prow, and a deep bloody scratch on Mael Duin's left hand, from his thumb to the end of his forefinger. In his closed fist it would make a circle of blood to match the eye.

He appeared to sleep, but there was tension in him, in the outstretched arm, down the line of his cape to the bent knee. I had seen that concentration in Nuca, and finally knew it myself, making a small piece of magic. Everything extraneous spins in the chest, then rushes down the legs and arms and out. Breathing slows and the world sinks down like a wave inside. That is the prepara-tion—the making room for something else. I had seen it before in Mael Duin, when in complete stillness he sent the stone ahead of the throw, so it was only its shape that followed, like the shadow that follows and joins the oar when the lake is still. In a contest there was a moment when he and the stone agreed before where it should fall, and now he was trying to send the curragh ahead, by his own power.

It was close to dawn when Mael Duin woke me. It was still too dark to see anything outside the boat. I could hear the mast creaking, the ribs of the curragh breathing against the ten thousand knots of skin, and something else, a slow rhythmic sound, that was familiar to me but at first elusive. Then Germane sat up and said, "The rocks—"

Light came and we drifted through a white cloud. Everyone had weapons in hand. The sound of the breakers was close now. Mael Duin stood, holding a long oar, ready to push us off a rock. Large white birds with black wings were wheeling in and out of the cloud like scythes. There were more of them every moment. Then suddenly we broke out of the cloud.

It was a small island, with rings of steep rock going up into sharp spires like a fort. The whole island seemed to be covered with white flags. Their fluttering sound rose above the sound of the sea. But the birds were mute. As we drifted slowly nearer the sand, we watched them open their great wings, take off, circle the spires and land below the cliffs, never uttering a cry.

Mael Duin shouted, "It's alright! I know where we are!" and he leapt out of the curragh and began to pull on the prow rope. I jumped out and caught up with him. "It's the Little Skellig, off the Iveragh Peninsula," he said, yelling into the wind. "We just drifted south. Tomorrow we can row west and we'll catch the Vikings by dusk."

We pulled the curragh up on the sand and made a camp in the rocks, then went to work repairing the mast. Germane checked the seams in the hide for splits and rubbed wool grease over the hull. We filled the water jars from a fresh stream up in the rocks, and killed enough birds for our dinner and two more meals at sea. Ardan and Cailte plucked and cleaned them, drying those for the boat on the rocks with salt. Their flesh was sweet and tender, like partridge. We finished most of the beer and all of the mead that night. The birds moved to the rookery above us when we settled in around the fire. Their elongated shadows, with drooping heads, were thrown out against the cliff walls. When the wind died down there was an occasional flutter of wings, then silence. Long ago, when Nuca and I were sleeping in a ditch or a field, he would sigh like that, or stir a last time, and then I'd know he'd gone into deep sleep.

I remember that night I was playing jackstraws with a pile of small bones when Mael Duin sat down beside me. "I heard once that druids can pick them up without touching them," he said. I told him about one who could do it: the high druid of Alba, who lived in Bonny Doon. How his lover, a shapechanger, taught him. She held her hand over the pile and the bones flew up. In her hand they turned to tiny weapons made of precious gems.

Germane and Cailte got drunk and argued about some calf with two heads that Germane had seen at a market in Galway, and Cailte called him a liar. Then Brian told a story about his great-grandmother Macha, how she saw an elephant drinking from a pond where she did her wash. It had little eyes, he said, and ears like mainsails. Cailte went to sleep, and Mael Duin walked down to the water. When he came back he spat into the fire, and said, "When he's dead, with his red beard stuck on his own blade, what will I do with him? Throw him out on the beach like a putrid jellyfish for the gulls? Bury him? Drop him into the sea? It's a great shame that he's so stupid, after all. Light eyes, like a weasel." Then after that, we let the fire go out, and slept.

We left the island early the next morning, our mast repaired and strong enough to take anything but a gale.

A red seal came up next to our boat just outside the rocks. It swam along beside us, then dived and came up with a small salmon. Mael Duin laughed; he was pleased with the good omen. He ordered Germane to steer northwest, and we rowed with the sun on our backs.

By midday the sky was flat and pale. There was little difference between the sea and sky to mark the horizon, just a smear of light green below a mass of blue, a blot of white for the sun and a single gannet hanging above. The mast shadow had disappeared completely. Only a small circle of shade came under each chesspiece from the game that went on perpetually below the mast, turns taken up by two men as they rested from the oars. The mast shadow on the waves had grown past the prow when Germane called out that land was near. We all looked where he pointed and saw nothing but waves lurching up and down. Then the curragh slipped up the side of a wave and we saw the small patch of land behind it. There were no towers or cliffs or trees on it—it was not much bigger than our curragh from that distance—but there was something moving, something alive on it.

It wasn't a man. It could only stand upright for a moment, then it would go down on all fours. We rowed quickly towards it. The animal could see that we were coming. Germane and Ardan thought that it was a horse, shipwrecked or abandoned by some boat in trouble, but I thought it was a big dog, maybe a wolf-hound, from the way it moved. Over and over it rose on two legs, leapt in the air and then ran back and forth across its bit of land like a dog crazy to see its master coming. Brian leaned out over the gunnel, calling the animal and clapping his hands.

Mael Duin called, "Hold your oars!" The sun was right in front of us, blinding. We drifted closer. Then Germane leaned on the steering oar, and the boat turned. The animal laid its head down between its front feet. Five lengths from the beach I could see its ribs. At four I saw the row of curved blue claws on each foot. At three lengths it pulled its lips from long teeth in a sneer and rose up on its back legs above us to an enormous height. We turned and rowed hard, and the curragh was battered with stones and sand.

When we finished bailing sea and picking rocks out of the boat, Cailte said we were lost, and Mael Duin didn't know where we were, and how did we know he hadn't made up the story about Little Skellig? Ardan said we should turn east and sail home, before we got destroyed in another storm. Everyone started to argue, but nobody said anything about the beast, until Mael Duin said if we were so afraid of a starving animal, how were we going to attack Vikings, and he was so ashamed of us, that he should have ignored the druid and done what he intended from the first, to go alone. No one answered him. We passed around the water flasks, took out the birds we had killed to eat, but they were spoiled.

There was no wind that afternoon, but the clouds got dark and dense and then it began to rain heavily, straight down on the sea, into the curragh. Two men were needed to bail. We strung our leather sails, blankets, and the extra hide tarps over the mast ropes. We moved everything into the center of the curragh, and Mael Duin said not to touch the inside of the blankets, or they would leak.

I remember that it wasn't so different from being in a small crannog on the lake during a summer storm; only the open triangles at the prow and stern showed the sea. But the chesspieces kept sliding off the board, and soon it took several hands to keep them in place, and no one could be certain where a rook belonged. Then Mael Duin wrapped the pieces in a cloth, put them away, and passed around a cask of poteen.

Immram curaig Mael Duin. . . that was really the first night of our voyage. Mael Duin was our perfect captain. He sang us the beginning of the Tain Bo Culaigne in his deep voice. Wrapped in his cape he sang, hugging his knees with the black sea behind him, and the indigo wool roof above. The lamp swung with the boat, making his forehead and his hair gold, and a violet hollow at his throat. When he finished Cuchulain's battle teaching, Germane, on his left, took up the song. We went around the boat, the cask following, each man taking a turn. The rain kept up, beating its dim rhythm on the roof. We were shoulder to shoulder along the gunnels. One by one we dropped out and slept, but I myself took Cuchulain to the ford.

Cuchulain saw the trap before it caught him, saw it and knew it for what it was. All living things must follow the ogam stem from birth to death. But dreams move backwards and forwards, and who can tell what is memory or vision? I heard Mael Duin begin to sing the death of Cuchulain and I dreamed of the hag, the washer at the ford, the goddess of the third face.

I dreamed that it was dusk, and I was looking into the dark east sky. Germane was humming one part of a song over and over.

She was out on the waves, bent over her washing, her back towards me. I saw her wring out a shirt and a cloak, then slowly lift up a knife, inspect it and carefully dry the blade. She worked away at something I couldn't see for a long time, scrubbing and polishing. Then she raised her head and looked back over her shoulder, as if she'd just become aware that she wasn't alone. I saw her searching the water, her eyes meeting, then passing, my own. She went back to her scrubbing. I looked away just for a second to see if anyone else was watching, but Mael Duin and Germane had their backs turned, facing the west. When I looked back she was gone.

I looked along the wake towards the stern. The clouds were churning like smoke rolling off a drenched bonfire. Suddenly she was there again. This time she was looking straight at me. She seemed very old, her eyes red-clouded. She put one finger to her lips and then turned full towards me. A dead man, a young man, lay across her lap, his neck draped over her arm. He was naked, and his many wounds were clean. When she had finished showing me she turned away. The curragh seemed to pull away and the distance grew between us. Then the sea was dark and empty again, and Germane was still humming his tune.

Then I woke up.

All down the boat men were sleeping. The rain had let up a bit and tapped softly on the blankets above us. Mael Duin and Germane were still awake, talking quietly. I watched the small patch beyond Mael Duin's shoulder, a patch of rain-flattened black sea, letting the dream ebb away. When the rain let up there were waves again, first black and smooth then tinged with silver as they rolled. The clouds were breaking up at last. There would be a full moon tonight. The prow was rising up behind me, arcing into fullness. We were going over. I opened my eyes and the boat leveled off. The rain had stopped, and Mael Duin was listening to Germane. "Then the fighting was over," Germane said. "I don't remember too much, except that he was about my father's age. I was kneeling in the grass beside him, my sword stuck in his chest."

"He was still alive?" asked Mael Duin.

"Yes."

"What were you doing?" he asked.

"I don't know. Waiting. I...had to get my sword back. He was looking at me. I was waiting for him to die, for his eyes to change. Then his leg started moving, a spasm. He was hurting badly. I held his leg down—I held onto his boot. When we were boys and Diuran got so sick, I wished it was me instead of him, because I knew I wouldn't die. Because of how his eyes looked—and this man—I was touching him, and he was looking at me. I thought he knew everything about me. But then he was dead, and then—then I couldn't get the sword out.

"Maybe I wondered what would have happened if I hadn't—if I'd held back my sword. For a moment I couldn't remember why I'd done it."

"He would have killed you," Mael Duin said.

"But then I saw someone I knew, and we grabbed each other and were so happy. We were both alive, and it was the first kill for both of us."

They didn't talk much more, and when they fell asleep I put out the lamp and lay down again, but I couldn't sleep. I tried to guess how far south we'd come, and then how far west again, and a group of stars shaped like a shield kept fading and reappearing in a different quadrant of the sky. At the same moment that, in anger, I realized it was too late now for sleep, it struck me that there was no such constellation. Then I must have drifted off.

I remember that there was a crash and brilliant light, and then I was lying on Germane, who was struggling and kicking. The tent above came down in one piece, collapsing on us. The curragh had run up against land.

It was a large flat rock, with two stone slabs on end supporting one across, like a dolmen, in the center. An

113

animal slumped toward us, dragging its huge body up onto the dolmen. When it was settled, it rose and swayed from side to side. When it stood still, I could see the muscles and bones churning inside. And then the skin alone moved in waves over its huge body. It had no legs or arms, but a kind of face with eyes above, nose and mouth below in the mass of folds. Two gigantic teeth came down over its jaws.

We got the boat free, pushing off the rock with our oars, and just turned when the animal spilled itself into the sea beside us. It came up next to the steering oar, opening its jaws wide and bellowing. It rammed the curragh hard, once, but we got one wave between us, and then three, and we didn't see it come up again.

We rowed west all that day and saw nothing but a small group of black rocks sticking up out of the waves, with a flock of gannets resting there. The white birds flew west and east over our heads. Only twelve of us needed to row at once, to keep a good pace. But except for taking turns at the steering oar, or keeping the fire alive in the big kettle under the mast, there was no place to go in the curragh, with twenty men on board. Since we had so little room to ourselves, it was easier not to talk. So when it was my turn to rest I stayed in my seat.

In the days that followed I learned not to think of anything but the sea. I'd hang my arm over the high gunnel, dipping my oar into the sea and taking it out with no force. Sometimes I'd lift the oar straight out, and let the water spill across the blade and over in one piece, like a sheet of fresh water coming off a flat rock. Or I'd turn the handle slowly and let the drops fall, some running together and some alone, making their own print on the sea.

But sometimes my oar brought up strands of sea grass,

like my mother's big stirring spoon in her kettle, bringing up fennel and onion shoots from the bottom. Maybe there had been a storm under the sea, and what lay across my oar blade was debris. At home after a bad storm there were always torn branches and leaves all over the lake the next morning. Or else the shanachies—the storytellers—were right, and it was mermaid hair. It looked like hair, but not as much as the current-combed reeds in the river that flowed into our lake.

The mast creaked as each wave went under the boat, and I thought of another small sound that had once kept me awake, that had made me get up from my bed in the crannog and look out the door. But it was only an old tin scabbard, caught up in a small backwash, hitting the lashed reeds again and again. It was bent and not worth fixing. It had never been fine enough to take to war. A good one, of iron or bronze, would have stayed at the bottom of the lake.

Sometimes, in Connaught, when kelp comes into shore in great amounts, the tide comes in red, and no one eats shellfish or whitefish for days afterwards because of poison. One evening, the sea looked brackish. When Germane pulled up his oar under the lamp on the mast and it was stained dark as rowanberries the birds leave to rot and split on the ground, we were afraid. Mael Duin stood by the mast, watching the sky, giving directions to the helmsman. The wind and current were southwesterly; we raised the sails, and put our oars away. There was no end to the dusk. The light made everything one color. Each smudge of dirt or crust of salt on our faces, necks and arms was a wound. The sea was calm, and the wind light. No one talked.

Then, directly below the setting sun, we saw land, a small island with low, flickering hills. We took down the sails, and rowed past the breakers. There were horses fighting on the beach. It was getting dark fast, but I could see their bodies shine with blood. Mael Duin said, "Let's move in closer," and we let the curragh go into the sand.

A horse swerved away from the boat, staggered and lunged towards the animal closest to him. He grabbed it with his hooves, and buried his face in its neck. He held on. Finally he threw his head back and blood spilled over his chin. His teeth had taken a broad strip of flesh away; muscles gaped in the other horse's shoulder, then the wound filled with black blood. He kicked its neck hard. It went down, and he turned on the next animal. Then it got so dark that I lost track of him. The grunting and panting seemed louder then. Someone lit a lamp in the boat. The animals stopped. Their shadows stood out sharp on the sand; bright blood shone on their hides. They shut their eyes against the light. Mael Duin put out the lamp, and we watched them fight.

Somewhere the Vikings were waiting for us to find them. I was glad. It seemed that if I could only think of the right word, I could reach across the sea and crush them. Mael Duin had his cloak off. He leaned over the side and put his hands into the sea. He drew them out and looked at them, dripping over his thighs. He smelled them, and tasted them, and then streaked his face, his chest and thighs with blood.

Before dawn we must have drifted away on a lateral wind; our anchor rope was broken, and the sea was right again, green-blue and choppy. There was no sign of the island. We had three fishnets in our curragh and flax line with good sharp hooks, but all day they came up empty. The gannets refused to take the spoiled meat we had from the hooks. When the sun passed over the mast

Germane came down to me and said we'd have to go back. The Viking island was behind us now, and we couldn't keep going west forever. Cailte was right—Mael Duin had made a mistake. We had to go back, we were almost out of water.

So I climbed down the boat to talk to Mael Duin. He was working on a piece of rope, twisting the flax and dipping it in the sea. Light cast up from the water was moving on his face.

He said, "Look, Diuran, how clear the waves are. Like green glass. You can see deep ocean in the top of each wave, the crest as wide as my hand. I know what it's like down there. Dark and cool, like glass on your skin when you have a fever. The green waves move across, one after the other like harp strings, but without sound.

"Everything down there moves slowly. Down there my thoughts turn over like a bright scarf—half animal—half flower. How could anything live up here? Nothing but bones. Bones like straw, feathers and leaves. Shadows that wheeze and puff their breath of smoke. Even the shadows are real below. You can feel them and you can feel light. But you can't be afraid of drowning, or try to breathe. You have to be like sand when a wave hits it. Lie still until it leaves you, cool and clean. Every child when it sees the ocean for the first time runs up to the tide and runs away. We shouldn't be afraid of it." He shook his head, and said softly, "Maybe deep ocean is our real home. They're still out there, Diuran. I can feel them."

I looked away from the sea, sick of its movement. There was a small, white cloud far over the horizon, perfectly flat, as though it had been woven into the sky. It cast a shadow on the horizon. I put my hand over my eyes and looked harder. It was no reflection.

There were the cliffs, the tower—I showed Mael Duin.

Southwest, off our bow. He turned back and yelled, "That's it! Drop the sails. We row!"

Germane at the tiller was grinning, shaking his head. I stripped off my shirt and put my oar into the water. I matched Brian stroke for stroke. The pull from shoulder to arm to back was a smooth stretch and the wind was fresh on my face and arms. I could feel the boat moving fast under us. She was a spear dividing the sea behind, the Viking island on the point of her prow. When I looked back I saw the skin bag bouncing against the mast with each jolt of wave.

We couldn't risk coming up below the tower again; Mael Duin said that the best plan was to beach the curragh and hide up in the rocks until dark, then go around the tower and attack. The sun was low when we made the cove on the far side of the island. There was no ship, but far back up the sand under the cliffs stood several pavilions made of black iron. The structures swayed very slightly in the offshore breeze. We watched from the curragh, but the beach was deserted. They would probably be back before night. Our luck was holding.

Mael Duin and I brought the curragh up onto the beach and everyone carried out weapons and boots. I sat down in the sand, broke the leather lace at the top of my boot and had to get back into the curragh and find the hide thongs we'd stowed with the extra hide, flax thread and rope. I was still relacing my boot when most of the crew was halfway up the beach to the cliffs. Brian was yelling something, but it was hard to hear him because of the wind. Mael Duin and Germane were setting the last stone in the curragh. "There's something up there," yelled Brian. "In the cliff. I saw something move."

We couldn't see anything. Mael Duin said it was

probably a goat. He tossed his cloak over his shoulder and walked past me. I could see them starting up the cliff, their weapons tied to their belts. The sun was breaking over the cliff edge and for a moment I was blind. There was a row of small cave openings just under the cliff edge. In the last hole, in a bank of shadow, something looked out and went back in.

"That's not a goat," I said.

"Come on, Diuran, let's go," called Mael Duin. The crew was moving up the cliff, finding hand- and footholds. It looked out again. It came out of the hole, all the way out, and another one right after it. They were huge ants. They poured out of the rocks. They lined up along the ledge, their eyes as big as fists.

Mael Duin screamed, "Get back to the boat!" In the dunes around us pockets began to open up and sand poured down like water. Out of the pockets came black sticks that grew to legs as the dunes shifted and the ants came all the way out. They swarmed over the boat, eating the ox-hide hull. Mael Duin ran to the boat, and was covered with ants. He got the boat clear, and we dragged her down to the water. Mael Duin stood waist-deep in the sea until Germane, the last man, got in. There were ants hanging over the tiller, but Germane got the steering oar out of the frame, and the boat began to turn. On shore the iron pavilions were moving. They were coming apart, breaking up and climbing over each other down to the beach. They came down to the water, more and more of them until not a patch of sand was visible. But they stopped at the tidemark.

Our boat was badly damaged. Four men bailed constantly while the holes in the hull were patched and sewn. That night the sea was purple and silver, a sweep of purple cloud in the west like an arm. When a quarter moon came up over the dark slip of the island, Mael Duin was already asleep in the prow. Germane lay with his head on my knees. I drank a little water and went to sleep.

It was very dark when I woke up. Mael Duin was leaning over me, his hair falling over his eyes.

"Where is it?" he whispered.

"Mael Duin? What?"

"Give me your knife, Diuran," he said.

"My knife?"

"Shhh! They're sleeping. We're talking too loud."

"You need to cut something?"

"Cut something? You know," he smiled at me, "Diuran, you're making it hard. No, nothing." He laughed. "What did I say? Just give it to me." He looked away. "Lie down and sleep, Diuran. Can you sleep? I wish you would sleep now."

"I'm awake now." I sat up.

"Sorry. I didn't mean to wake you up. That's right, isn't it? See, it's there." He pulled my arm. "You were lying on it. Your knife." I put my hand over the sheath. "What's the matter, Diuran? Give it to me."

"I don't know," I said. "What's wrong with you?"

"Nothing. Nothing's wrong. It was fine—everything was fine." He laughed a little, embarrassed. "I'm dying, that's all. Don't worry about it. It doesn't matter. Everyone does. It's alright. I have to. I think it's been happening for a long time. That's it, isn't it?" He gasped, then smiled again. "Yes. Give me your knife."

"I will," I said, "in a minute. Sit down beside me."

"It was a trick, wasn't it? I didn't see it. Why didn't I see it?" he said. Germane stirred at my feet, turned over and was still.

"You wade out and try the water; it looks so cool, then

the dark wave comes over you, and you can't touch bottom anymore. The shore is a long way off, and the sun's going down. It's getting darker.

"I'd forgotten. It was there when I was a child, in the fold of my blanket, in the corner of my room, in the dead stag's eyes—in the hollow, spiked branches of his crown. It was in the sound when I blew the whistle, a piece of his crown.

"Now it's inside my mouth," he whispered, "and my fist, and a cave, watching from all the dark places, waiting to be let out. The holes keep getting bigger, the holes in the leaves, too, ripping the skin away with your hands, leaving the bones red, yellow, brown, nothing but crust; it turns to dust in your hands.

"It's there underneath, too. Under rocks and one blade of grass, under the cornstalks, a whole field of dark. The scythe is coming and it's not heavy. It never was, for me, not even when I was a boy. Don't you feel the weight of it now, Diuran, under your shoulder, your knee—here, in the crease of your arm? Close your eyes and you can see it, the dark field right there under your eyelids, with midsummer fires.

"It comes back every night, over and over, draining the green out of the trees, the blood out of a cow. It looks better that way, her hollow cheek more beautiful than life.

"The sea is full of dark, coming apart in the water, drifting and turning. A tooth under a flower, a hand, the fingers spread out tapping the sand for eternity. When will it be over? When will it be over?" He got up. "Go to sleep, Diuran, I'm busy."

"What are you going to do?"

"Nothing."

"I don't believe you."

121

"Her horns are up. Look at the moon, Diuran."

"I see it."

"Shall we look? Can we look? Shall we see him, the father? Better the father, than the . . . other. What was that? Here, let's make room for the hero, his beautiful eyes, no woman can resist him, no sackcloth disguise him. Take him down for me, Diuran."

I unhooked the bag from the mast and put it in his hands. He opened it and the skull rolled out, down into the boat. It rocked between two willow ribs then stopped, the smooth forehead shining in the moonlight.

"Like a pear," he said, "a moon-colored pear, only the size is wrong, isn't it? Just like before—oh god, what's that—what's that coming out of the hole?" He started tearing his face, and his eyes, and I grabbed his arms.

I screamed, "Light the lamp, Germane, light the lamp!" and held Mael Duin's arms back, the pain shooting up my neck and down the middle of my back, but he still struggled and I didn't let go. The light came on, and I saw the blood streaming down his face, and I yelled at him, "There, it's there—look at it; it's only a skull. There's nothing else. The ants are gone. Look at it." He looked at the clean eye sockets and screamed.

"Mael Duin! Pray to the goddess! Listen to her words! Always look into the dark—there is something looking back at you. Look, Mael Duin—the ants are gone. Death is not the end. Call on the witch of darkness, Mael Duin!"

"No! Not her!" he screamed. "Stay away!" Then he shuddered, and cried "Father!" And the boat was deathly still. Up and down the boat everyone was awake but frozen. The sails, half-wrapped around the mast, stirred slightly. Germane kicked his blanket over the skull. He put out the lamp and sat down beside us, all three braced against the boat. The gunnel rose and fell against a sky of the same color. I could feel the boat breathing and bending under us.

Then I saw him, up on the mast—a huge bird with a curved beak. Mael Duin suddenly relaxed in my arms and closed his eyes. Germane was looking at the mast, then moved his eyes to the sky and down. He saw nothing. The bird took a piece of the rope in his beak, dropped it, then opened his wings and lifted off the mast. After a moment Brian came closer to me, and others began talking softly down the boat.

"What happened?"

"Nothing," I told him. "A bad dream. Go back to sleep."

"It's getting cold. And darker. The wind's changing."

"Make a fire. Then go back to sleep."

I put my hand against Mael Duin's throat. His pulse was fast and hard. Moonlight seemed to go through him; the ash ribs of the curragh lined up beneath him. The pale light washed the curve of his forehead and eyelids. I saw the crescents of dark under the lashes, the marks of pressure or stain. I saw that the cut on his hand wasn't healing. "Wake up, Mael Duin, wake up!" I shook him.

Germane looked at him and said, "His eyes are open."

I let his shoulder drop so that his head lay in the crook of my arm. He stared, his eyes as dark as the eyes of a man pulled too late from the sea. He turned his face away and said "Never mind." I let go of him and he crawled to the other gunnel, sitting across from us with his knees up. He pulled the end of a blanket towards him and the skull rolled out. It stopped on an ash rib by my foot.

"Here," said Mael Duin, "give it to me." I picked it up and reached it across, turning the eye sockets towards me. He pulled it in and covered it with the edge of his blanket. "The wind's changing. Northeasterly. Put up the sails. Tell the crew we're going home."

5

That night we had a strong following wind coming out of the northwest, and there were stars to reckon by. I took my turn at the tiller, and kept the North Star on my left and let the huntress go straight over my head. When Mael Duin took my place at the helm, the leather sack tied to his belt again, I could say nothing to him because I was glad we were going home.

Germane sat beside me. Near dawn a flock of birds passed over, calling, but it was too dark to tell what kind they were. "Summer's done," he said, "the dark is lasting." We watched the east, as if we were boys again, waiting for a flock of geese to come into the lake. When the sky began to lighten, it picked out a narrow stream of clouds along the edge of the sea. The sun broke and the cloud bank turned gold. Then, suddenly, there was blue sky over a ridge of pale green cliffs.

Our wind kept up and the steep cliffs of Clare jumped closer. It seemed like they were walking towards us out of the sea, while our curragh with its full sails stood still. Mael Duin ordered us to take down the foresail before we hit a coast wind. Our mast could take a wind but no gale. But we came through the fine mist with our mainsail flapping. The cliffs were dark and high above us. The limestone went straight up with a thick edge of green turf at the top.

We came right into the beach, a quiet stretch of sand with coils of kelp above the tidemark, and terns hopping in and out of them. We beached the curragh, then half the crew went to work getting a fire started in the shelter downwind of the curragh, and the rest of us stalked the kelp mounds with flax line and a piece of wool-greased hide on a hook. It had been two days since we'd eaten. I had five fat gannets hanging from my belt and a handful of wild garlic when I reached the fire.

Germane was kneeling over the steaming, fragrant pot, stirring the meat with his spear. Cailte was standing behind him, touching his face, asking how could he eat with his mouth bleeding. Brian told him to be quiet, and to help clean the birds if he wanted to eat at all. His mouth was raw, too, like the rest of us, from salt and wind. I finished the birds and took my knife to the garlic, dropping the peeled segments into the black pot. "That's garlic," said Cailte. "Is that something the druid taught you, while he was telling you how to find a Viking?"

"I like the taste of it," I said.

Germane said, "So do I, and if you have any words to add with that, go ahead, but you aren't keeping this first batch aside for some sacred purpose. I'm starving."

"It's hard being a poet, eating other people's food, when they're not as smart as you," said Cailte.

"Stir that," I said to Germane. "It's scorching. These are the fattest birds on the beach, and they were trouble, too, taking their time with the bait, so if you need privacy to finish your work, Germane, just tell me. I got pleasure snapping their necks, and I could do it again, for Cailte here, just to keep my hands warm."

Cailte looked straight at me and touched his mouth. Brian knelt suddenly by the pot and put his head down. When he looked up he grinned and said, "I thought I was going to faint. I'm that hungry."

Cailte looked down the beach where Mael Duin was walking in and out of the tide. "I thought he was going to faint when he got out of the boat, he was shaking so hard. I heard what he said last night." Then he made a point of lowering his voice. "His real mother was crazy, you know. That's why Fedelm had to take him."

Germane took out the spear he was using for a spoon, tapped it on the lip of the pot and raised it to Cailte, holding it steady. A fine rope of smoke slanted away from the point. Then he skewered two birds and let them drip on the sand.

"I'm going up the cliff—see where we are," he said softly and went past us.

Brian called after him, "Look out for the Arans." Germane nodded and waved, his back to us, and kept walking towards the cliff.

"We should be south of the burren here, by the look of these cliffs, but the Arans will tell us." Brian stirred the pot with his own knife. "These are almost done. Who's going to cook?"

I put a stick in and took out two birds. "Not me," I said. "It's warmer walking."

Cailte said, "He's going down to Mael Duin. Save your meat, poet. You don't know Mael Duin these five years. I saw him in Cashel; he was crazy. Just leave him alone. He'll starve if he wants to. There's nothing we can do." He laughed and took the knife away from Brian. "Let him go back to the Eoganacht. They think he's a hero. He won't have to do anything to prove it."

I put my hand on Cailte's shoulder. "You're getting too thin, Cailte. What are you looking at, Cailte? Look at me." I brought him closer. "You'd be dead now if Mael Duin hadn't pulled you out of the water. You never were a fine swimmer, were you, Cailte? You'd better hope that he eats something. He's keeping you alive still, maybe." I let go of him and turned my back on the fire. Walking away I could hear him complaining to Brian, "What's wrong with him? I don't have to listen to him anymore; we're home," and Brian telling him to shut up.

I walked down the beach, dropping the clean bones as

I went. Mael Duin was ahead of me, walking fast in the hard, soaked sand. When he turned and came back, we sat down and I told him that Germane had gone up the cliff to get a sighting of the Arans. I put the second bird between us on the scrap of cloth I had. He didn't touch the meat. He twisted a shell in his hands so the sun streaked along the edge of its spiral, turning the smooth pink to gold. I watched the breakers come in. The lip of tide went out with its broad hush and then it was quiet. Down the beach Cailte was talking with Ardan and Seamus. Waves broke somewhere far to my left, and echoed off to my right, *boom, boom,* and then the two sides came together and the sea burst in a roar. "That's a real storm brewing out there; maybe coming in tonight," I said. "We're lucky to miss it."

He said, "Diuran, you don't need to watch me."

"Winter is on us," I said to him. "It's three days now I've seen the change in the sea. It's time to come in."

"Past time," he said. "Diuran, do you know the creature that makes this? Have you ever seen it?" he said, tracing the rim of the spiral from the outer edge into the center with his thumb.

I took the shell by its smooth spikes and shook it. "It's empty."

"Dead," he said, "out there." He pointed to the blue and gold rumpled water. "You see how the wave curls in on itself, then breaks. It doesn't travel, it doesn't go anywhere." He swung the skin bag that was tied to his waist up into his hand and took the shell back with his other. "You could have a hundred cows for each hand if these were gold. They're the same weight." He pitched the shell high and far into the water; I didn't see where it went in. The tide went out again and he said, softly, "Keep your bones, we have enough of our own." Then he started back up the beach. I caught up to him and he said, not looking at me, "You should find something for the sacrifice."

"Will you go up the cliff with me first, Mael Duin? You know the shape of those islands better than any of us." He said nothing so I asked him again. "Will you come up with me?"

"You should be tired of company, Diuran, after so many days in the curragh." Then he turned away from me and started off, his stick leading into the sand.

The wind was hard at my back, but it was slow walking in the sand. When I reached the cliff wall Germane sent the rope down to my hand, but I didn't touch it. Nuca had taught me to fear them. "You think of nothing but the rope, a thing you have made, and forget the living rock. The rope sets you against the cliff, as surely as a boat with a wooden hull will set you against the sea. But if you think of the cliff, how it binds stones and how it lets them go, how it holds itself hard against the sea and wind, you will never fall."

Germane pulled me over the top, and we stepped back out of the wind. We were standing at the edge of an open meadow. There was an island of high grass in the middle, and the wind, when it came, blew tunnels through it. Along the treeless ridge the grass was trampled and broken, but there were no signs of cattle or sheep or any other animal. Rusted helmets were scattered everywhere, and there were depressions in the sand and grass where shields had fallen, but not one remained, taken perhaps for their ornament or weight of bronze.

"Was it Vikings, do you think?" asked Germane.

"Maybe. This is a natural harbor, the way we came in on the current with no trouble. But there's no fort here." I looked at the sea. White clouds were rolling at the horizon; I couldn't tell if those were islands or deep storm clouds behind. On the beach below most of the crew were resting, and farther down, Mael Duin was walking by the water.

"If it was Vikings or an ancient Irish battleground," I said, "it's a peaceful place."

"It's quiet, and safe—if only Cailte would go drown himself."

There was a quail trilling in the grass by the stone. We were so far above the sea that we couldn't hear the breakers. I made a row of five ogam notches on my staff—five marks for the first day of our voyage—and Germane lay on his back, feeling the solid earth under him.

After a while we got up to look over the far ridge. I started running towards the mound of high grass. Germane came up behind me and kicked one of the helmets across my path. It rolled into a clump of weeds and stopped. I reached in to get it out, looking back at Germane, and the feel of it in my hand made me stop.

"What's wrong?" he called, coming up beside me.

The thing was coming apart in my hands. "Metal doesn't rot."

He took it from me, and said, "Do you remember when we were small and played summers by the cromlech back of Fedelm's house? We had armies—the Firbolg's and the tuatha below—and they all had helmets, little caps, like...helmets made of hazelnut shells..." He dropped the thing in his hand. I reached down to take it and looked up at the same time, past him.

At the edge of the field the grass was blown flat against the ground. A huge black cloud like the gigantic head of a horse appeared above the cliff. The wind struck with gale force. I grabbed Germane and we ran for the cliff.

I took hold of Germane's shirt and we crawled over the

cliff. I kept hold of him all the way down, and we never slipped though we went down fast. We touched sand together, and I let go of him. Then I picked up my staff that I'd dropped from above and ran for the sea.

Mael Duin was ordering everyone, getting the boat down into the water. Cailte was yelling at him, "You're crazy, we can't go out to sea in this storm—it's suicide!" Brian was screaming, "The Detsorach! The horses of hell!" I climbed into the stern, and Germane after me, grabbing Brian, yelling at him over the gale, "What did you see? What did you see?"

He yelled, "Mael Duin saw them come out of the water and take the cliff." We had no time to tell him about the shield- or hoof-shaped marks in the turf, or the giant hazelnut shells. We pulled on the steering oar but it was jammed fast into the frame. Now the wind was blowing spray all the way back up the cliffs. I kept working on the oar but it wouldn't move. I turned to the prow; Mael Duin was straddling the gunnels, letting the sail out. Cailte was below him, clutching the prow and screaming into Ardan's face: "We're going to die! Don't be a fool! It's his curse. He's crazy." There was the whole length of the boat, men and oars, between us. Trapped in the stern, I saw Cailte knock Mael Duin into the surf with his oar and jump on him.

The tide came back and Cailte was sitting on Mael Duin's chest, one hand yanking his head back by the hair, the other holding a knife at his throat. Mael Duin was looking right at him, and his face was relaxed. He was going to let Cailte do it. He was pulling away from us, spiraling away inside. Cailte moved. Mael Duin's knees drew up and his eyes went dull. Cailte had cut his throat. Now he would back away, and I would see Mael Duin's blood running out.

As I put my hand on the gunnel to leap into the sea I saw Mael Duin seize up and the knife fly out into the sand. Cailte screamed and Mael Duin had him fast with his arms bent behind him. When Mael Duin turned him into the boat Cailte's left arm was hanging limp.

Then Mael Duin pushed Germane away, yelling something about the mast. He grabbed the steering oar with both hands and shook it loose. The boat came around and we faced open sea. The sails filled, and then a blue-black mountain of a wave rose up to the mast. It stretched higher and higher until it burst and drenched us. Germane and I bailed in the stern. Mael Duin stayed at the tiller, pulling and leaning on the oar, heading us into the face of each wave as it rose. They were coming too fast, with no pattern or direction to them. The curragh shuddered as each one rose under and dropped us. I saw no horses in the deepening mass of waves that grew huge, broke and joined beside me.

Before the sun went down the land was out of sight. The sky was folded like cloth in bloody streaks. There were patches of clear sky with stars coming out, but the waves kept coming. Mael Duin let ropes out behind us to slow us down. Sometime before dawn, when he couldn't see to steer, he poured all the wool grease we had left on the waves around us, to quiet the waves. Daylight came and the sun never dried our clothes. Dark and cold returned and no one slept or spoke, but the boat did not go over.

On the morning of the second day the wind dropped. Germane let out our mainsail and we stowed the bailing buckets. I tied Cailte's broken arm with strips of linen. We took some rest at last. The curragh rocked. There were big waves plunging up and down as far as we could see, storm clouds in the east. A wave off the bow fell, and behind it lay an island.

Mael Duin shouted from the stern, "Let's get out of the wind and dry off. Take up your oars."

I said, "We can sleep," looking from the churning black clouds behind us to the sloping towers going up and down around the island. "That storm coming will be on us before dark."

Germane said all he wanted was water to drink. Mael Duin climbed over us. He sent Germane down to the tiller, and got down on the seat beside me. He put Germane's long oar into the sea and fell into the stroke.

Germane kept us heading toward land. Gradually the sea moved down the cliffs, showing more and more of the face of the island. A wave went down and there was a dark place in the cliff, the shape of a door. When the tide went out, and the cliff started to pull us in so we had to backpaddle hard against it, we saw a narrow, protected strip of sand between the high rocks and the cliff itself.

"There it is, if the rocks don't destroy us," I said to Mael Duin.

"Look at the birds," he said.

Up in the cliff, far above the sea, were thousands of gannets. A wave rolled in and broke, and the spray reached up and kept the lip of the shelf shining wet. When the water pulled away from the cove, the birds dove and skimmed the pools. They flew back up with fish flashing in their beaks to settle in the cliff.

Mael Duin counted the waves. Somewhere, in the interval, there was one that would give us the longest quiet, the best chance to get into the cove before a breaker built up and came down on top of us, or crushed us between the wall and the rocks. The seventh wave is always the mildest. We kept our position, just rolling on the surface. Then Mael Duin yelled, "Hold your oars," and I took my oar out of the water. The boat slid forward one length, two, and he yelled again, "Back!" We rowed against the tide. "After this wave!"

Germane screamed something at him. He nodded and motioned with his arm, then took up his oar.

Behind me Brian said, "Here it comes—" and I turned around. The stern rose up, so that Germane with the tiller in both hands stood high above us, equal to the mast. Then the wave went under the boat, and for a moment I looked down from a height. Then it passed the bow and started climbing. The rocks disappeared, the door and the cliff, then suddenly the sky was dark and it flew apart. Drenched, I started to row, hard. I couldn't feel the boat moving forward at all; it seemed to be sliding back out to sea. If we didn't go ahead now, before the sea turned again, the next wave would destroy us. Then I felt the boat move and we cut across the underside of the wave. A big rock with the sea pouring off it loomed up ahead, and then was suddenly behind. We slid past without touching it at all, and down into the little harbor.

We skidded into sand. The wave came in. It destroyed itself on the barrier of rocks and only covered us with spray. We tied the curragh up to an iron hook driven into a crevice in the cliff wall, and left her floating in the backwash. We walked in file behind Mael Duin along the narrow strand toward the door, keeping the cliff wall at our left and the luminous wall of fog on our right. I couldn't see past the breakers now, it was that thick. There was a piece of shiny bone coming through a hole in Mael Duin's skin sack, which bounced off a rope at his waist. We came to the door and stopped.

It was high enough for a man to ride through on his horse, made of heavy black timber like the beams in the door at Cashel, but smoothed by the sea. Cut into the bottom, level with my knee, was a small gate that opened and closed when the waves hit it, gushed through and went out again. There was nothing to see inside but dark water going through the trap, since night was coming on quickly now.

I could hear Cailte, halfway down the line, talking. "I'm not going in. It's stupid. Mael Duin's crazy. You're crazy too, if you follow him." Germane sagged back against the wall and shut his eyes. I stood by him and waited for Cailte to pass. Up ahead Mael Duin raised his fist and swung it against the door three times. Nothing happened.

Cailte said, "Just because there's no boat tied up outside doesn't mean there's no one in there. You don't know what he's leading us into. I could take the boat around to the lee of the island and wait out this storm, if I had some help."

Germane said, "If there were two of you in the world, Cailte, we'd all drown ourselves this instant, without your help." I put my hands on the rock, one on either side of Cailte's face, and spoke into his ear. "If you say one more thing this day, you'll hear words from me that will raise six foaming boils on your face, and twelve red, seeping sores on your back, so that we won't be able to stand either side of your face. No one touches Mael Duin's curragh." I turned back to the door and Mael Duin was gone. The tide hit the trap, went through, and came out again. I stood and watched it move the gate until I decided to go in after him, and then the big door opened and he stood there, with a lighted torch in his hand.

"There's no one here. I've got a fire started," he said. We went through together, the last man pulling the door closed. It was quiet and dark. A wave hit the door behind us, and I could feel water running across the floor. Deep in the room a fire burned low. Mael Duin held up his torch and we followed him, staying close to the bare, high walls. There were three steps up and the floor was dry and cold. I ran my shin against something hard and stopped. It was the edge of a wide cot, with dry blankets folded upon it. There were more of them, laid out in the middle of the room, and in the center one deeply carved bed with silk sheets stretched across it. Then Germane found a low table before the fire, with food wrapped and piled upon it, and someone else found casks of mead.

Germane, grinning like a starving wolf, cut the gray crust off the cheese and put a thick slab into my hand. There was a boom, and a rush of water against the wall below, and Brian said, "The tide's coming in."

The sea was hitting the door harder now. Mael Duin got up from the table and walked out of the light. In a moment he came back, drained his cup, and said, "The storm's on us. I'm going to sleep."

"I'll take first watch," said Germane.

"Sleep. Let the sea take it. No one can get in as long as the storm's on. Let you all rest now." Mael Duin set his cup down and disappeared into the dark. It was soon after that I found a bed myself, with Brian and Germane lying down beside me. I was still feeling the sea, but the wine began to work. I don't know how long I slept.

I remember first the sound of the wave falling against the door, then dim light coming above and behind from a long, narrow window, high above the hearth. The stone walls of the chamber were a soft grey, nearly green, and covered, I thought, with a silk or fine linen that stirred with the breeze. Then I saw that it was just light playing on the bare stone, light coming off the water. Germane was still asleep beside me. A wave hit the door and I sat up. Salmon came in with the stream of sea that shot through the trap. When the water went out again, the fish remained. Brian watched the gate, crouching by the door with the sea swirling around his knees and the walls rising high above him. Every time the sea came in the door, salmon came with it, and the woven basket beside him filled quickly. I lay down again and closed my eyes. There was silence, then the wave falling against the door, moving across the stone floor, and a soft hush as it retreated.

Sometimes there were low voices—the bed moving as someone changed position, and always the dark. I remember half waking and wondering about the fire, because whenever I stirred I saw the glow of it first. But then when I sat up the walls had the soft light moving on them again and there were only glowing coals left in the hearth. Everyone else was asleep. I found a stack of dry turf and some kindling stacked under the high window. I made up the fire, then took a cup of beer, some cheese and a blanket, and sat against the wall by the hearth. I noticed then, for the first time, that the walls were not rough stone, but carved, all over, in elaborate spirals. The whole surface of the walls had been picked out, with a fine chisel, and the spiral designs stood out against the rough background. I followed the path of one spiral; it led me to a second and a third. I couldn't find one that didn't connect with another, that failed to return, but the way each connected was never repeated. Sometimes a new path would begin within a spiral the way a flower unfolds, from the center, or simply, like a blade of grass. Or else they came together like a snake lying along a branch.

The spirals were cut into the ceiling of the room, too. At that great height I kept losing my place, tracing them, and my head began to ache. I lay down on the floor, with the blanket under my head, and my empty cup next to my hand. A small spiral hung centered over the cup like a delicate flower in a vase. I traced the spiral with my finger into the center, back out, and into another spiral.

When I closed my eyes, I discovered that I could still follow the design by staying on the smooth path and know when I was getting off the track if the tip of my finger bumped over rough stone. When I traced a spiral to its center, it seemed that my finger was actually moving deeper into the wall, but when I traced it out it came back even with the surface. Every time I reached the center of the spiral a wave came against the door and into the room, and when I traced it back the wave went out again. Then I realized that the spirals would keep going even if I put my hand down, my wrist getting tired, and that the wave coming in and out actually moved the spirals.

Always, when I woke, the light had changed. I would get up and walk around the room, put wood on the fire, then sit on the floor and watch the sea come in the gate and draw away. When I was hungry I would roast a salmon on the fire. I saw how differently each man slept—how deeply, and the length of the interval between each breath. I saw Germane fling his arm across Brian's shoulder, Brian turn, and Germane follow him, like a wave, and how some moaned or sighed and maybe dreamed. Mael Duin, lying alone, stretched out long like a dead chieftain on his rich deathbed, never moved or made a sound. I couldn't tell if he dreamed or not, but his sleep was deep. Sometimes I sat on the floor against his bed, looking at the strands of colored wool in his blanket, the way a purple next to a blue strand made it disappear; when a green lay across it, the blue thread would rise.

Once when I awoke I saw Cailte standing over him, his arm still in the sling I had made. I watched, without moving, with my knife in my hand. When he slept again I got out of bed and stood over him for a long time, but in the end I knew it would not be enough. I would still hate him, and he would still be dangerous. At least he would not harm Mael Duin while I slept. I put the gesa on him so that he could not touch a sleeping man, as some cannot touch a dead one, or a snake. Then I went back to my bed, and when I heard someone moving in the room, I could follow my own sleep, and dream.

There was a sharp edge of light, and something moving in front of the light. A low cry, then another. There were gulls flying past the window. The sky was blue and bright. I turned over and saw that the bed was empty beside me. All the beds were empty. Mael Duin was standing under the window beside the hearth, talking to Germane.

"The storm's over," he said to me. "Come outside and look." Mael Duin leapt up the narrow stone steps towards an open door at the back and top of the chamber, which I had never noticed before. I followed him, and Germane came after.

The light outside was dazzling, and the wind was fierce. I stood at the top of a natural fortress. The cliffs made a steep circle around the small island, with a wooded glen in the middle and the sea a blinding sheet of light surrounding us. Brian sat on his heels skinning a rabbit; the ground around us was honeycombed with rabbit holes. "How long did I sleep? How long did the storm last?" I asked.

"Come down here, out of the wind," said Mael Duin. There was a shelf in the rock. Mael Duin, Germane and I sat with our backs against the cliff, looking over the top of the island. "What do you call the brown thrush that winters in Ireland and goes north in spring?" he asked. There was something different in his voice.

"Sacan."

"I've seen three flocks come into the meadow this morning." He sat with his bare arms folded on his knees, the skin sack at his waist.

"So we are not far from home," I said.

There was a silence.

"Maybe not," said Germane. He rubbed his beard, looked at me and looked away.

"Mael Duin has agreed to go back," I said to him. No one spoke. The sky and sea were blinding; the wind roared. I could only see the silhouette of Mael Duin's head, turned away from me towards the water.

"He...tried," said Germane. "Now we have rested. Things are different here. Diuran, you have to tell us what you think...what you feel now. I don't want to try those cliffs again—that look like something and are not. You saw the shells, and the hoofmarks."

"Hoofmarks? I saw the marks of shields. I saw a storm cloud. The Arans were cloud-covered," I said. "One day's sailing, into the east—"

Germane stopped me. "Diuran, we're lost. We're deep into winter—"

"No," said Mael Duin. "It's not just winter. I thought it was better to go back, but I made a mistake."

"You had no choice."

"There is no choice," he said simply, as though he were telling us a fact. "There is no wine here, there is no bread. We can never go home until Ailill Ocar Aga is avenged."

I thought, how can that be true? He can't know that. Germane wouldn't look at me. I knew he read my thoughts: Mael Duin is mad, how can we trust him? It seemed that the wind would shake the cliffs under us, and they would fall. "We are in the hands of the goddess," I said.

"Nothing will stand in our way now." Mael Duin stretched his arms out and smiled. The tide broke against the cliff below us. I heard the ringing of iron against iron. Then I thought, this is also an island.

Germane told me his plan. "There's no reason we can't winter here with the sacan," he said. "We replace our mast, watch the sea and the birds. When the first flock goes north we follow them. We'll surprise the Vikings before they sail. They would never suspect us of trying what they do to us. No Irishman has ever sailed a curragh like ours. And this is a safe place. There's food and fresh water, and a turf bed below the ridge. If the winter is harsh we can't get out, but no one can get in, either."

"We can capture the sacan and make cages for them," I told them, "and take them aboard the curragh. That's how the Vikings get their bearings. When we get past landsight we let them go, two each day until we find them."

Mael Duin stood up. "Let's bring the boat inside," he said.

So we tipped the curragh on her side, brought her in

through the door of the cave, and turned her over, belly up, as we do the small curraghs above the tide. The tide ran under the black hull and out again all that winter. She slept quietly beside the door, and often entered my dreams. I never dreamed about the islands, but most often of Nuca and some thing we had seen together or some piece of ritual or poem he had taught me, and we would be back in Erin. The dream would always finish itself in the cave, with Nuca there, and his goat legs and his dark shoulders naked in the heat of the fire inside, and behind him, in a corner of the chamber, the black boat.

At first we slept, and took walks alone. Mael Duin threw spears in the glen. But after a week we began seeking each other out. At night we sat around the hearth roasting salmon or rabbit and talking, while the waves touched the wall outside and retreated. I worked on my staff, cutting the ogam strokes into it as I made the story of our voyage. Germane often sang and played the small harp he had. I rarely saw him during the days, which he spent alone, diving for seal in the small lime-stone caves on the other side of the island. It rained frequently now, and when it rained seals always came into the caverns. Our supply of grease for the hull and dried meat for the voyage grew as winter passed. When it rained hard at night we covered the window and our chamber grew hot. Smoke spilled out of the hearth and filled the room.

One wet night we stripped and sat on the edge of the stone floor, taking turns cutting each other's hair. Mael Duin used my father's knife. He reminded me of the time he'd cut my hair, and we'd been punished and sent to bed on the eve of Samhain. "There was a thrush up in the smoke hole," he said, "making her nest up there, and she kept looking down at us, pulling pieces of thatch out.

I wished she could pull the whole crannog down and then we'd escape...and never come back. You looked terrible."

"But you told me I had beautiful hands," I said, remembering.

"Let's see them."

I held my hands up. There was silence. "Well?"

"It's nothing; I just remembered my dream." He laid the knife down and sat beside me. "That's all; I'm finished," he said, looking off into the smoke.

"Tell me," I said to him. He turned toward me. The black orb in his eyes shrank back away from the sapphire. "What was it?"

"Nothing at all. It was dark. There was water in front of me, black, with rings spreading out. I touched the water, and then I was under it. For some reason your hands reminded me."

Then Seamus said he'd dreamt about Fedelm again.

"I wonder how long they watched the coast?" said Ardan.

"Not long, in an Daingin. Someone drowns off the Blaskets every week, maybe every day in winter," said Cailte. "Besides, they thought we were all crazy."

"Twenty bodies coming up on shore would be something unusual, I think, Cailte," said Germane. "Something worth repeating. Fedelm knows we're still alive, believe me."

"She knows we haven't drowned, but we could be dead. Killed by the Vikings," Cailte argued.

"I'd rather be cut in half than drown," said Brian.

"That's because you've never lived by the sea," said Germane. "You'd get used to the idea."

"Not used to the way they look when they've been in there awhile," said Cailte.

Germane said, "Who cares, if you're already dead? I'm not afraid of drowning."

"You don't mind at all, if your enemy goes before you," said Mael Duin. Everyone turned and stared at him. Brian told a dream he'd had about the red-haired Viking. Germane picked up his harp, and said, "If it were up to me, I'd take a slice from a Viking sword—there's no faster death. I got hit with the edge of an O'Malley blade near Achill last winter, and I was bruised for a month." We laughed, and then he sang. His voice was warm and clear.

Mael Duin wrapped his arms around his knees and listened. He would let the talk move away from the Vikings and try not to bring it back himself. I knew, though, that they were never out of his mind, and that he waited, while we rested, until the year turned and the days grew long again.

Soon after that Mael Duin and I went together down into the glen to choose an ash for the new mast. Brian had a forge going under the cliff. He had mended weapons and made a new ax. Everybody else was hunting. Salmon were scarce now but the rabbits and goats were plentiful. We found the small ash grove easily by the grey bark. Now that the leaves had fallen, everything was visible: nests in trees, holes and tunnels in the ground and in thickets. As we walked I thought about how other things became visible in winter, and how those things frightened some people and attracted others, but that Mael Duin, who had always been the most intolerant, was the most vulnerable. Whatever happened would happen to him. I was sure of that, on the island, but I didn't know then how she would take him.

We found the best tree and Mael Duin went back for the ax. I started clearing the brush around the tree so that we could carry it out. Then Germane suddenly broke through the tangled brown grass and thorns. He was naked; I gave him my cloak and we walked back to the chamber. He was getting ready to dive, he told me, in the small cave on the west side of the island. He saw something, some rings in the water. He waited for the seal to surface again. Then it came—a wall of water—he didn't know where it came from. He got out just before the whole cave was drowned.

There was no one in the chamber except Mael Duin when we got there. He listened to Germane and said he was lucky, and we decided not to talk about it with anyone else. It was getting late in the winter for seal hunting, and the next night water froze in daggers from the trees, and the ground was hard. Nobody went to the caves again.

The nights grew longer and longer and we began to mark the change in the beam of light from a small crack above the door in the chamber. Every evening, if there was a sunset, the beam started across the floor in a slow swerve left, shortening its reach as the weeks passed. Then it grew no less for several days, and began to swerve right, and each night took a little bit more of the floor into its grasp, until finally, it reached the wall and touched the rim of a spiral.

Then we saw the first sacan take off and return several hours later, and the next day some did not return. Woven baskets were made for those we would take on the boat, and the baskets were filled. That night Mael Duin made a sacrifice of a young goat. He held its head against a stone bowl with cup marks in it that stood beside the stairs. He thanked the goddess for hospitality, and asked for a fast and successful voyage. Then he cut the animal's throat. He brought the blade down its belly and the

146

shining guts spilled out, heaped on the floor in a series of perfect, interconnected spirals. Everyone stood close around. Steam rose off the entrails, turning, as it must, against the sun.

What is the meaning of the spiral? Water draining and steam rising, the coil of a snake, a shell, the vine. From hidden places men have watched the sky turn, and stars move into a center and out again, creating new worlds. Their knowledge survives in the carved stones. Nothing is random. Only death is accidental. Nuca believed that in the spiral all things are connected: the killer and his avenger, the chieftain and his men, kin who share the boat to seek the killer.

Mael Duin said, "It is the ancient sign of the Eoganacht."

"Death . . ." said Brian, softly, "and the spiral that returns is the spirit coming back. Vengeance."

"It is my father's name," said Mael Duin. Everyone drifted away from the stairs, getting their weapons and clothing ready for the voyage, and Brian put the goat on the fire.

6

Adcess an bith imbith n-ingnad os ler lindglass.
And wonders were seen in the world on the blue ocean.

Mael Duin, with his father's skull tied to his waist, drove us north in the triple-hide curragh. We sailed to islands that no Irishman had ever seen before, nor would any believe, if I told all the truth.

There was a small island with a brass fence running down the middle of it. A shepherd kept a white flock of sheep on one side, a black flock on the other. He put a white lamb over the fence among the black flock, and the lamb turned black; he put a black ewe down among the white sheep, and the ewe turned white. From the curragh Mael Duin threw a white, stripped oar into the black sheep. The animals parted and ran from it, and the oar stuck up straight in the turf, like a spear of black iron.

Dub la findu co ndath gessi,
Find la dubu co ndath.
Black among white has the color of a swan,
White among black has the color of coal.

It has always been that way—poets must disguise the truth to be believed, or feel shame if the story is too harsh. Afterwards, people said that it was the thirst and hunger and loneliness that made us see things that could not be. Many blamed Mael Duin and his madness. But if he was mad, it was not the kind that sees things that aren't there; Mael Duin was blind to everything but his vengeance.

I know these islands well—the marks on my staff. The

island of the burning river, the island of the blacksmiths; they are true as the notes of a song. You will know why Mael Duin banished music from Tamlacht. But if you cannot believe them, then you will not believe that Mael Duin became abbot in this monastery, or that a man can change. You cannot believe in the simplest thing.

We were moving fast. There was a powerful current under us, and the wind was behind us. We let one of the sacan go; it circled the boat, and took off straight before us. So we knew that the current was taking us north, to the Viking home. Seamus caught some gannets with bits of seal fat on a flax line, and we had fresh meat to go with our hoard of cheese and mead from the cave.

After sailing for many days we saw the shape of a fort against the night sky. There was no light on the island, so we dropped anchor below a bridge that led from the rocks to the door of the fort. At dawn a soft breeze came up; it blew from the island and smelled slightly of oranges. The fort was gold with morning light. The bridge was like a span of ice, transparent in places, so the green sea showed beneath, and then opaque, like mica, where it reflected the sky above. We needed fresh water, so we put on our armour and our weapons and left the curragh. But we couldn't walk up the bridge. It was steep and as slick as ice.

The sun was hot, and we were tired from so many days at sea, so we rested at the foot of the bridge, keeping our weapons beside us. A girl came out of the fort, carrying a pail. She walked halfway down the bridge, lifted back a slab of the bridge, and filled the pail from the pool below. She put back the cover, and when she reached the door Germane called out, "Let Mael Duin be made welcome!" But she went in, and the huge door closed behind her. Then the bronze swords and spears that hung upon the door moved and made a sound. A feeling of longing came into me, so strong that only sleep would ease it. When I awoke, the sun was just coming up from the sea, and the mist was rising off the pool and the bridge over it. The girl was getting water again from the well in the bridge. Germane held out his spear and shouted, "Let Mael Duin be made welcome!"

She said, "I have heard of the strength of Mael Duin." Then she went in and the door shook the weapons hanging upon it. And the sound was a wave that brought sadness and sleep down.

But when we woke the next morning, the girl was standing at the foot of the bridge. She was dressed like a queen in the old songs. The white mantle that covered her shoulders was like swan's down, edged with red gold. There was a simple, wide gold circlet around her yellow hair. Her skin was pale, and it showed through the white membrane of silk she wore under her mantle. Her feet were purple-white, bare in silver sandals. She took Mael Duin's hand and said, "My welcome to you, Mael Duin. I have been waiting for you."

She showed us a path cut into the rock farther up the beach. The scent of oranges vanished as we left the cove, and there was only the smell of salt. The sea was wild and spray rose high against the cliff. We followed her up to a large stone house that overlooked the sea. There were beds wide enough for three of us to sleep in, and one bed with sheets of white silk for Mael Duin. He asked her who owned the house, and she said that there was no one else on the island. She knew nothing of Vikings; she had never seen their ships.

She gave us food; I couldn't tell what it was until I tasted the sweet flesh of fresh oranges. But Germane beside me had venison, and Brian, hazelnut cake, and it was clear that although the food was the same, and looked like curds, each of us tasted something different, perhaps what we loved most. When we finished eating, she served us cups of shining liquid from her pail. It looked like plain water, but it made us drunk.

That first night Ardan said that Mael Duin should take her, but she left the room, and didn't come back. The second night, after she had served us, Germane got up from his bed, caught her wrist and said, "Don't go away. Why don't you stay here with us tonight? You could sleep with Mael Duin." She said that she had never slept with a man, and she ran out of the room. We searched the house, but it was empty.

When she came back the next evening, we drank and said nothing to her while she served us. Then Mael Duin put his arms around her and touched the white silk and her white skin under it. She shook herself free from him, gently, saying that tomorrow she would give him an answer. He said that they could waste no more time, that the Vikings would not wait for him, and he touched her waist and her breasts. She showed no fear of him, putting her hand on his shoulder, and she said, "Wait. One more day, and then I will tell you the secret of the island." So he let her go.

That night I dreamt that I was sleeping high up in the limbs of a huge orange tree, and the wind was moving the branches around me. In my dream it began to rain. I woke, and there was rain falling on my face, and arms, and on all of us, in the curragh. We were on the open sea, with no land in sight.

> Three stones for the triple goddess who made the
>   world:
> The cloud, the wave and the hill.

One for the girl with the golden hair
One for the mother
And one for the old hag who tricks you and gives
you your death.

Our new mast held before the wind, and we filled all
the flasks we had with rainwater for drinking, but it was
hard sailing two days in constant rain. We were glad
when we saw the high limestone walls of a rath off our
bow, and we went ashore, armed, to look for shelter. As
we walked up to the ringfort, the rain let up. It was very
still inside. There was a large courtyard overgrown with
new grass and masses of purple and white flowers. Shoots
of rowan were starting up under an ancient, gnarled
rowan tree in the middle, whose branches bore few
flowers. Houses made of the same white stone faced the
courtyard, their windows bare, the roof thatch gone. We
followed Mael Duin into the largest house, whose broad
doors stood open. With the roof gone, and the sun
coming out, the house was full of light, and we could see
everything at once. There were four limestone pillars
inside the main room. A small white cat was leaping
from one post to the other, watching us from above.

Treasure covered the standing walls. There was a long
row of gold and silver brooches with their pins stuck into
the plaster. Below that hung royal torcs, the treasure of
kings, neckpieces of pure, thick gold, smooth or twisted,
all of plain and perfect design. Swords with massive hilts
of gold and tarnished silver hung below. Beyond the
main room were smaller rooms with chests of dry quilts
and garments placed beneath each window. And behind
the house, in the separate kitchen, were jars of poteen.

Some time past midnight, after everyone had gone to
bed, I got up from my pile of quilts and went outside to

look at the stars. I couldn't sleep, and I thought it was because the moon was full, because I can never sleep with moonlight lying on me. I walked into the main room and saw Cailte standing in the shadows. We had the same thing in mind, to look at the treasure of the house. Neither of us had wanted company, but Cailte had seen me and I couldn't leave or deny my presence. So I walked up to a plain gold torc, incised with the shapes of the sun and moon, and took it off the wall. For a moment I half expected something to happen, some sound to break the silence and wake the sleepers, but there was nothing. The white cat sat on a pillar, licking its paw. Cailte came to my side and took hold of a magnificent sword hilt.

"Who could be so rich?" he whispered.

"No one."

"So rich that he could leave all this unguarded. Maybe he's dead."

"I'd like to believe that," I said. "But this is Irish treasure."

We put the torc and sword back, and left the room. I didn't sleep until late, when light was starting to come into the sky. Then I heard sounds outside the window, and Mael Duin was standing by my door with his back to the main hall, talking to Cailte and Brian.

Cailte said, "I'll take one of the gold necklaces, Mael Duin."

Mael Duin said that he must not, that the place was not without guard.

"I see no weapon on you, Mael Duin," he said. "You're captain, and while we're at sea we will obey you, although you have gotten us lost, and we'll never see home again, or Vikings. But I have a right to the treasure, and so does everyone else. They won't like to hear this. You'd better find yourself a weapon, or will you take those from us too?" Then Cailte walked out of the house, with Brian after him.

Then Mael Duin said we would waste no more time, that it was time to sail, and he went out of the house. The crew came into the courtyard, with their weapons drawn. Cailte walked past Mael Duin into the house. Mael Duin started giving orders. Cailte came back out. When he reached the middle of the courtyard and passed the rowan tree, coming toward us, I saw the flash of gold on his neck.

The little white cat ran after him, and as it leapt towards the tree with its claws out, he screamed. The cat went right through him, like a burning spear. When we reached his body we saw the glowing red hole in his chest, his black charred eyes and hands. Mael Duin picked up the torc. The cat walked around Cailte, keeping on the white stones. Ardan aimed his spear, but Mael Duin grabbed it out of his hand, and the cat followed Mael Duin into the house. He put the gold back on the wall. When he came out he told me to take Ardan and Seamus down to the boat.

We built a pyre on the sand. Mael Duin brought Cailte's body out of the rath, and laid it on the pyre. Then we drank the rest of the poteen. We did not go back into the rath, and we left the island when night fell. As we rowed away the bonfire played on the white fortress walls and turned them to fire. Ardan said, "He's burning," and the keening began. We marked our sails with black ash from the gannets' bones, for Cailte, and rowed all night. The next day we saw nothing but sea and sky. We let two more sacan out of their cage. They perched on the cross rope just below the swinging leather satchel on the mast, then took off straight north.

That night we heard flocks of birds in the distance, and the sound grew louder the next day. At dusk we saw the island come up over the edge of the sea. When it was dark Mael Duin ordered us to arm ourselves and go ashore. We needed food and fresh water.

It was hard walking through the thick woods of yew and cedar and tamarack with only moonlight to see by. Birds sat in the bottom branches and in the bare places in the middle where the foliage had died. They were tall as vultures, with shabby brown and black plumage. Branches and foliage were covered with pale excrement. Down clung to the green-black bark and lay on the ground under the trees.

We were getting ready to turn back when we found a small clearing. There was an old stone well in the middle, with coins, bones and long, speckled feathers on the ground around it. A rancid smell, like sulphur, came from the well. We heard something move in the trees on the far side, and backed into the woods with our weapons drawn. There was nothing in the shadows beyond the well. An owl in the tree in front of me swerved his head around and blinked. Then Mael Duin touched my arm, and I saw something white moving in the trees. An old man came out into the clearing. He was naked, with long white hair and a beard.

Mael Duin stepped forward and said, "We are men of Connaught, on our way north. Who are you?" The man peered at us, biting his lip. He scratched and picked a flea out of his chest. He looked at the ground and shook his head. "Are you alone?" asked Mael Duin.

He said, "I am a man of Erin." He had beautiful clear blue eyes.

Mael Duin sat on the edge of the well. "How did you get here? We saw no boat."

"No, no boat here. Only yours. Sometimes I see Viking sails, far off. But not yet. Not yet. I am the only man here." We went down to the beach, where the curragh was anchored, built a bonfire, and shared our last jar of poteen with him.

He seemed lonely and anxious for us to stay. He asked questions about our voyage, but Mael Duin said only that we were seeking our fortunes in the north, and could not stay long. Then the old man turned to Seamus, asking him simple questions about his home, his animals and his family. He had a soothing voice and a gentle way about him. Germane said there was something about him like our grandfather, who taught me poetry, and died when I was six, and listening to the old man's story, I thought of him, and of Nuca, and I had no wish to sail farther north.

The old man said, "Let me tell you the truth. When I was young I wanted to leave my family and discover my power. I set off alone in my curragh, and when I got just a little way out, my boat split and came apart under me. I swam back to shore, and then I cut a piece of green sod from the land and tied it to the bottom of my foot. I stepped on it and it carried me out to sea.

"A long time ago it sent roots down into the water, and became a real island. You can taste the water from my well for yourself; it isn't salty. And the well gives more than water. On Friday and Wednesday it gives whey-water, and on Sunday it gives milk. On the high feasts of the year it gives wine. But every day I have half a loaf and a morsel of fish from that well. I am never hungry. Do you believe me?

"Each spring a new tree comes up. Do you see these beautiful birds? They are the spirits of my children, my family. The spirits of my own boys and girls, my wife, my brothers and their wives, all here with me. We are together.

"Tell your chieftain that if you keep on your voyage, two of you will never reach your country."

When the old man said that, Mael Duin got up slowly and picked up a sword that was lying in the sand beside him. He walked over to Seamus and gave him the sword, saying, "Take this to the curragh. Then get her ready to sail." A look of panic came into Seamus's eyes. Mael Duin said, "You leave Cailte behind now, and remember him again when you've got a Viking sword at your ribs. Go on. We're wasting time."

Seamus begged him, but Mael Duin's eyes were hard and he turned away. When Mael Duin looked at the old man, it was as if the place where he stood was a patch of bare sand.

I got up and went to him. When I started to speak he told me to get to the boat.

We took up the anchor, and the old man touched the hull at the stern and said to Germane, "Sail west." Mael Duin turned around in the bow and ordered "North!" The old man stepped back on the sand and laughed.

Germane pushed us off and we were back at sea. Seamus sat huddled under his cloak and wouldn't speak at all. We kept the North Star off our bow all that night. The wind was behind us, and we were moving fast. By the evening of the next day we saw another island, but I think if we hadn't been out of food, and needed fresh water, Mael Duin would have passed the land and kept going north.

At the first light we rowed into shore. There was smoke rising above the trees. We armed and went into the woods, moving cautiously. A sudden movement in the upper branches, or a moment of too-deep stillness, might be our only warning of Vikings. We followed a stream to a clearing, where a large stone mill, with smoke rising from the roof, stood beside the water. There were narrow black slits between the stones at each of the four levels, where an arrow or a spear might be poised.

There was a loud crack and the massive wheel shuddered. A trap in the top of the trestle opened and the water poured out. The wheel began to turn, creaking. On the left side of the mill was a black timber door. Mael Duin walked along the stream, past the wheel, and went in the door. Soon he waved to us, and we followed him in.

It was dark inside. The sound was deafening. The floor shuddered and the low ceiling beam vibrated under my hand. The churning millstones were as high as my shoulder, deeply pitted from the tiny grains of corn. The sound of the grinding was like a granite mountain turning. When the stones slowed and stopped, I felt the sound for a moment after, like the stroke of a drum or the low note of the harp that goes through you.

The miller was very old, his skin wrinkled and yellow with age and dust from the corn. He had a fire going in a small hearth behind him, and his bald head and neck were sweating, so that it seemed that pieces of his skull shone through the skin, and the veins in his neck stood out bare as ropes.

Mael Duin said, "What mill is this?" He didn't answer. "Who brings the corn to you?"

The miller looked at him, scowled, and spat on the dust.

"He's deaf," I said.

The miller grinned, and his eyes flashed hatred. "I hear better than you. A stone just fell into my stream."

"There's someone outside," cried Ardan.

We ran to the door. Seamus was walking on the grass below the wheel.

"There's no one there but Seamus," said Mael Duin.

"Who is Seamus?" he rattled. "Seamus. Seamus." He laughed. "Shame, shame, shame, shame, shame." When he laughed, his teeth showed, black and broken. He put his hand down into a sack of flour, and felt it, letting it stream through his fingers. "What are you doing here?"

"We're hungry. We have nothing to eat. Give us some corn."

"It doesn't belong to you. Go away. No one has cheated you. You've had more than your fair portion, and everyone knows it. You don't belong here. Get out."

"Who brings the corn?" demanded Mael Duin, bringing the flat of his sword down hard against the table.

The man leaned on a lever and the wheel stopped. He said, "Go outside and look."

We stepped outside and saw that the sky was getting dark. We had only been in the mill for minutes, and it had been morning when we entered, but now the sun was going down behind the mill. Someone was coming. We ran into the woods and watched. Into the clearing came crowds of people in dark robes, carrying sacks on their shoulders, and pulling wagons loaded with corn. They carried sacks into the mill, and then came out again on the other side.

"The dead! Remember the horses of hell!" screamed Ardan. There was a crash from the mill and the gate opened. Water gushed over the wheel and it turned. We got back to the curragh, rowed out beyond the breakers, then dropped anchor for the night.

There was less than a cup of fresh water left for each man, so Mael Duin ordered us to row along the island. We found a broad cove on the western side of the island,

and came in where the sea was clear and turquoise. Plain wooden ships without mastheads stood in the cove, each painted black, with two black sails and simple curved prows, sharp as spears. A steady drumbeat came from the land. There were clusters of small stone huts on the terrace above the bay. People walked slowly between them, and sat on the rocks above. They wore dark, hooded cloaks, and long, dark gloves, but no weapons.

Mael Duin said that he would go ashore and get water, but Germane said no, that as captain he couldn't leave the crew, and that he himself could go, or all of us. There was fear of going or staying in the curragh, and a feeling against Mael Duin that was poorly hidden. If the words had been spoken aloud, there would have been nothing to keep them from killing him. So I cut a piece of rope and we drew to see who would go, and it was Ardan who got the short piece. Mael Duin put his sword and shield on him, telling him not to go out of our sight. Ardan climbed out of the boat and made his way up the rocks. He walked along the top of the terrace and stopped at the first group of seated people. We could see them turn to him, but their faces were hidden. He sat down beside them on the cliff and they seemed to talk together. The morning passed and Ardan made no signal to us to bring the flasks. He didn't move from the bench.

Mael Duin opened the last cask of water and passed it around, then threw the empty cask overboard. "Go on," he ordered Germane, "get him," and then he threw a cluster of water casks after him. "Don't forget these." Germane tied the bundle at his waist, gave us a grim smile, and climbed out of the curragh.

He followed Ardan's path up the hillside. When he was close to the top he waved, and Mael Duin waved back. When he reached the path he stopped, swung the flasks behind him, and put his hand on his sword hilt. He walked slowly towards the bench where Ardan was sitting with the dark-robed people. He passed them without looking at them, went on to the next bench, sat down and put his head down in his hands. He didn't move.

Mael Duin shouted at him, but I don't think Germane could hear him over the wind and the drum. I said I would go up, that maybe he was sick. Seamus said he was going, Mael Duin too, and they put on swords and shields. Mael Duin tore a sheet of linen into three strips. "Put this over your nose and mouth when you get to the top," he said. "Maybe the air is poisonous. Don't look anywhere but straight ahead to Ardan. And when we get to Germane, take his arm but leave the water flasks behind."

When we reached the top of the cliff, we covered our faces and linked arms. The drum was loud, pounding out the keening rhythm. A group of people walked in front of us, their weeping audible, but their faces hidden. When we reached Ardan's bench, he wasn't there. The group of mourners still sat there, but Ardan wasn't among them. We went on to Germane's bench. He, too, was gone. A lone, robed figure sat there, his head in his hands, weeping. We stood behind him, and saw Brian waving from the boat. I looked down at the seated, veiled man, and saw the bundle of flasks tied at his waist.

"This is Germane," I whispered to Mael Duin. We grabbed his arms and stood him up. He groaned. We walked him down to the first bench, where Ardan and the others had sat. But there was no one there.

"Back to the boat," Mael Duin gasped, and we took him down.

We shoved Germane back into the boat. "What happened?" cried Brian.

"We lost Ardan," Mael Duin told him. "Look along the shore. Do you see him?"

"He's gone up the hill. He walked right past you—didn't you see him?"

"No," cried Seamus. "Then we have to go back."

Germane begged us not to go back. "You'll never find him," he said. "I saw their faces. Every man on that rock, all death's heads—don't you understand? Ardan was one of them, too. You'll never find him. You can't go back." Germane was shuddering. Mael Duin knelt down with his hands on Germane's shoulders, and talked to him.

"Germane, what happened to you?"

"I don't know. Is the drum still going, or is that inside my brain?"

"We hear it, too."

"I don't know what happened. When I got to the cliff I saw them weeping. And what they felt made sense to me. I forgot about the water, about you. I belonged there, with them."

Mael Duin said, "How could you believe that?"

"I can't remember. The drum was part of it. But mostly the people. What they knew. That seemed beautiful. Now it seems horrible. I don't understand. But I had to sit, and listen, and weep." His voice shook, and he wept. "Mael Duin, please, Ardan is lost—he's gone, I know it. Let's get out of here. Away from the drums."

Then Seamus said that we had to find water, and that Ardan would suffer less on that island than the rest of us would at sea. Germane hugged Seamus, and thanked him, crying. Mael Duin ordered Germane to take the tiller, and he said that the first taste of fresh water would belong to Seamus, and that when the division of the Viking hoard came, that the first choice would go to Seamus, for Fedelm, the mother of Ardan.

We picked up our oars, and watched the hillside as long as we could see it, then put up the sails and went north.

THE APPLE TREE

7

Two days out from the dark island we lost the current, and there was no wind. We rowed all night and the next day until dark, then the sky became overcast and we lost our bearings. Mael Duin said he would release the last two sacan at first light. We had no food or water in the curragh, so he had to set a guard on the birds. Each man brought his weapons with him when his turn came around, and sat huddled before the pot fire and the wicker cage. But the birds died from hunger, thirst or cold before dawn. When I got my share it was not the meat I craved, for the flesh was as dry as wood. But the bit of gelled blood was pure salt. I kept a bone on my tongue; it made my mouth water. Mael Duin took it away; he said it would make the pain in my gut worse, and drain the last moisture out of me. So I cut the silver button off my cloak and sucked on it. It worked better than the bone; it cooled my tongue. Still the heavy sky brought no wind or rain.

That night I piled sheepskins over Germane because he was shaking, lying in the boat. He was angry and told me to leave him alone. Seamus told him it wasn't his fault, that he and Ardan and Cailte should never have come, but that Mael Duin had some kind of power over them. He said they were all going to die, and his brothers wouldn't be alone. "They were right," said Germane. His eyes glittered. "We can't get back," he whispered.

Brian said "No, it's too late. We can't. Forget it."

Mael Duin spoke from the opposite gunnel. "I left him, Germane." His voice was like gravel. "I would never have let the curragh stay in that cove, not for a single night. Never. Not if you and Diuran were lost, not if any man of the crew was lost to the island."

"I don't believe you," Germane argued. "You took Cailte, Ardan and Seamus on the boat against the druid's orders. You saved them."

"You could have gone back and left us in an Daingin. And my brothers would be alive today," said Seamus. "But it was too much trouble; it would have taken time. Listen to him, Germane, nothing stands in his way. No man, living or dead, will keep him from the Vikings."

"No man, Seamus, only the sea."

"Where are they, Mael Duin?" whispered Germane.

"Yes, tell us, Mael Duin," said Seamus, laughing.

"Close. Very close now."

"Are they dead, Mael Duin?" asked Germane.

"Not yet." He turned his head, and looked out at the flat sea. His dark, heavy-lidded eyes narrowed, his gold hair lay close to his head, like feathers. "Death is close, but they don't know it." He swallowed and began again, whispering. "Their luck is running out. Look at the sky, Germane." The clouds were breaking up.

"No rain," murmured Germane.

"There are stars coming out," said Mael Duin. "Take the tiller."

"Shut up, Mael Duin," I said. "Stop torturing us."

He stood up slowly. I put my hand on my knife. He said, "Pick up your oars," and then he went down to the stern, and locked in the steering oar.

Germane doubled up, retching. There was nothing in him.

Seamus said, "Even Diuran would take this boat away from him now, but he can't. Nobody can. We're too weak."

Germane asked for water. "There isn't any," I told him. "Rest."

"Sea," he said.

"If he drinks the sea, he's dead," said Mael Duin.

"Don't listen to him, Diuran, he's crazy. It won't matter. I swear it," Germane begged.

Mael Duin put his oar in the water and started rowing. I dipped my hands into the sea and gave them to Germane, then filled my hands again and drank death.

I remember his face over me, the black orb of his eyes swallowing up the blue, the rims of his eyes wet. Mael Duin put his hands on my shoulders and shook me, hard, but I couldn't feel it. My druid training served me well. He was far away when he put his hand on my neck, and then his cheek against my lips; he was as distant as the small, round moon behind his shoulder.

Then I dreamt of the old woman on the waves. She showed me a man's body; it lay in the branches of a tree. His skin was white and dry as parchment. A wind came up, and he turned into a cloud of dust. A flock of starlings flew out of the branches. I called them by their true name, *druids*, but they wheeled away; they wouldn't come back and join together again.

I woke and thought that the mast had fallen on Mael Duin. He was motionless, with his arms around it, but there were dead leaves still attached to the tree. Then I saw the muscles in his arms tremble, and that he was alive, and that it was not the mast, but a huge, gnarled tree beside the curragh. Mael Duin held us fast to an island no larger than a crannog on Lough Corrib. The waves went under us, but the boat did not move.

He was talking to himself, arguing, his voice deep and hoarse.

"A trick of the goddess, or an error in judgment? Ailill Ocar Aga, having no future but death, left his son everything: madness and death. What for the mother? She told him the time was unlucky, so he gave her a brooch with apples in silver, for a child. A small thing, to him, a brooch and one night spent among his last nights, and what living thing doesn't give up its seed before it dies?

"But a pig will eat her farrow, and not for hunger. She knew her son, his madness like her own. When I was a fool, knowing nothing, I wished only to live while dreaming of death on a Viking sword. Now I believe in your vengeance, goddess. You pretend to give so much, then take it all away. You keep the Vikings hidden and safe in your hand. You teach Diuran to love you, but he follows me, and you kill him for it.

"No; I've killed him for it. I've lost them all. I've lost the Vikings; all these, in the curragh, who trusted me, are lost. Dead without water, and nothing but water around us. I am worthless to you, having nothing to bargain with. What do you want? Who are you?"

There was silence, then he answered, his voice broken with crying.

"Yes, I know." He spoke the words of making, that children say at games, but only the druids and the ancient dead knew the meaning and uses of them, spoken deep in the great stone sky chambers of Meath and Sligo. He spoke them softly, like words of comfort.

"I am a wind of the sea.

I am a wave of the sea.

I am a sound of the sea."

There was a breeze on my face. Mael Duin ran his hand down the branch, over the brown twigs.

"I am a stag of seven tines.

I am a hawk on a cliff.

I am a tear of the sun.

I am fair among flowers.

I am a boar.

I am a salmon in a pool.
I am a lake on a plain.
I am a hill of poetry.
I am a battle-waging spear." His voice changed, growing stronger, covering the roar of the rising wind.

"I am a god who forms fire for a head.
Who but I knows the secret of the unhewn dolmen?
Who but I knows where the sun shall set?
Who foretells the ages of the moon?
Who brings the cattle from the house of Tethra and separates them?
On whom do the cattle of Tethra smile?
Who shapes weapons from hill to hill?"

The wind blew the sails out, and the curragh leaped. The branch broke off in Mael Duin's hands, and the boat moved away from the tree. He ran his hand down the branch, and when the twigs snapped back up from under his hand, there were green leaves there, and red fruit.

Then his face was above me. I saw the marks of white salt in the creases around his blue eyes, and the wind was blowing his gold hair out like a kestrel's hood. He took the knife out of my belt.

"Diuran," he said in his rough voice, "stop dreaming now." He opened his hand and there, inside, I saw a full moon, clean and white, but rimmed with red and dotted with five black stars. He brought the knife up to his hand again, and put a piece of apple in my mouth. It was sweet and cool, and it took my thirst away. "Can you feel this?" He put the half apple in my hand. "Finish it." He went up and down the curragh, giving the fruit to each man. Soon we were seventeen living men. Germane sat up, asking what had happened. The bright sores on his mouth were fading. I told him what I'd seen.

"How does an apple have so much virtue?" Germane

looked back towards the stern, where Mael Duin was bent over the tiller. The rudderless boat was spiraling slowly on the waves, and the wind was twisting the ropes and the leather sails. He yanked the oar out of its frame and the boat straightened out. The sails filled again.

Germane told me that Seamus was drowned. He'd gone overboard during the night, while I was asleep. Mael Duin could not save him.

We went to work on the ropes; when they were untangled, I went down to the stern.

"You drank the sea," he said to me, then he put my hand on the tiller bar. "There's the current again; keep her on course."

He pointed north off the bow, shielding his eyes from wind and spray. There was a vague shape beyond his outstretched hand, the shape of a mountain lying in mist. It was exactly like Nuca had described to me in Connaught, the first island outpost before the Viking land. Then we knew we were in Viking waters, and prepared our weapons.

The shapes of the islands were familiar by Nuca's instructions, but what we saw there, no one had foretold. We reached the first outpost before dusk. It was a large rock, covered with burned heather, black stones, and tangled hazel brush. We sailed up right into the shadow of the hillside, with our polished blades on our knees and Mael Duin standing at the mast. There was no sound or movement from the rock, until a rock bounced down and people hidden above began to scream. Hazelnuts rained down on our shields and rolled between the ribs of the curragh. The sea around us was covered with them. We put all our nets out, and filled the curragh while the people on the hill, thinking we were attacking them, screamed and hurled nuts.

I saw no Viking weapons or helmets of gold on them; they wore the rough clothes, but there was no sickness or starvation on them, nothing to mark them from my own kinsmen but the misery of their great fear of us. They stared, they clutched each other, they screamed, and their mouths were black holes. They watched us as we rowed out of the shore wind and put up sail.

We ate our fill that night. There were strange stars that I had never seen before in the sky, and I wondered what shapes the Vikings saw in them. Two days later we made land again: a large island, with an empty beach, and a broad green meadow beyond the dunes, where a herd of large swine grazed and lay in the sun. Mael Duin killed a reddish brown sow. She was so huge that when she was stretched out on the spit, it took two men to turn the handle. I remember how Germane and I stood watching the juice drip down onto the rocks and the fragrant steam rise. Then Mael Duin threw the empty water skins down at our feet and told us to go find some water.

I got my staff from the curragh, and Germane took his spear. There was a stream in the meadow where the swine grazed, but it was muddy and slow. We climbed meadows for an hour or more, following the stream, looking for a place where it moved faster, or broke over clean rocks, but the water grew darker and bitter tasting, and then we came to a place where it disappeared into the ground.

We were tired and hungry, so we decided to climb one more ridge, and if we couldn't find the stream again, we'd go back. But there were trees growing close together down in the middle of the valley below, and we could hear the sound of the water. Germane went ahead, and I stopped to take off my clothes. The sun was hot, and my skin was caked with salt. I wanted the feel of fresh water. I left my clothes and ran barefoot through the trees toward the river. I came out suddenly on a high bank. The river was moving fast, and the sun was on it like a blast of gold. Germane was kneeling at the edge of the gorge above the water, examining the shaft of his spear. When he looked at me, his face was suddenly full of fear. He cried "No! Diuran—"

I swung my staff around but there was nothing behind me. Germane yelled, "The river—don't touch it! Keep back!" He grabbed my arm, taking me slowly to the edge. He lowered the blue-green shaft of his spear down until it went into the river. A trail of smoke rose from the blade. He took the spear out of the water—the tip was charred black. The sun went behind a cloud, and the gorge went dark. The river still glowed—a deeper gold than when the sun was on it, like turf in a hearth fire.

I went back for my clothes and we walked along the high bank, keeping a distance from the edge. We saw no animals or birds. For awhile the river narrowed as it dropped deeper between the walls of the gorge, and the trees thinned out and disappeared. Then at a bend the walls grew shallow, and soon they were nothing but stones along the shallows. The water was blue again.

The river turned and opened up into a meadow. There were oxen lying in the grass on the other side of the water. They were huge, hornless animals, with pure white hide. We tried to coax them across the river. Germane struck his shield with the flat of his blade.

The oxen rose up together like a white wave. Then a huge man stood up from behind a knoll. He told us not to frighten the calves. We went back to the beach and told Mael Duin what we had seen. We got the curragh ready to sail, hacked the pig into pieces small enough for our cooking pot, and quickly left the island.

That night there was ash on the wind, blowing into our eyes, and when the sun rose the next day, there was a small wooded island off our prow. From a distance the woods seemed to be on fire. But as we came close and anchored, we saw that it was only sunlight off the waves, moving on the bark, leaves and bright yellow fruit. There were strange animals moving under the trees. They had red hide, red eyes like pins of molten lead, and their short hind legs were thick and muscular. They would back up to the trees and kick the trunks hard, then feed on the fallen yellow fruit. At dusk, they disappeared into holes in the ground. Then the birds that had rested on the waves around the boat all day flew to the trees, and ate the fruit.

When the moon came up Mael Duin stripped and swam to shore, and brought back a bulging sack of ripe fruit. The ground was hot as a furnace, and his feet were burned. He said that no Viking or other man could live there.

"In the year of the Viking slaughters terrible portents appeared: exceptional flashes of lightning and fiery dragons were seen flying in the air..."

The image of dragons is carved on Viking boats, weapons and silver; it was said that dragons live in the Viking land, and they sleep underground. As we left the island the next morning it started to rain, and steam poured up from the trees.

The farther north we sailed the darker the sea—lapis blue and cold. One day we saw whales, giants that dwarfed our giant curragh. Mael Duin was stringing a boar's rib bow he had made. He put a spear into the string and aimed at a gannet, who was fishing some distance off the prow. It wasn't a shot any of us would have cared to try. Just at that moment two whales surfaced—two wave-washed, smooth-backed breathing islands. One of them gently nudged the hull, then dropped down into the dark. But Mael Duin made the shot. I didn't think they would harm us, unless, playing with our boat, they tipped us over into the freezing water. But Germane didn't like them—"viking watchdogs," he called them. Mael Duin laughed and reeled in his line. "They go north with the sacan, like us," he said. He laid the gannet on the floor of the curragh, jerked the arrow out its back, turned it over and split it down from the neck with Germane's knife. "The Vikings eat them."

Soon we were headed into rocks and mist, and saw no more whales. We had to go slowly, pushing off rocks with an oar. As dusk came on the mist dissolved, and then we saw the dragon boat. The small ship, with six oars a side, was moored between the jutting arms of a large rock.

"Keep the sail up. Let them see us coming," Mael Duin said, taking the helm. "Take two alive for hostages, unless these are our men. We need an escort to our enemy." The rocks parted. We drifted closer and closer under sail, but still there was no movement ahead.

"They must see us by now," I said.

"Yes." His voice vibrated like a struck shield. "They aren't going to try to escape."

I thought of the old woman on the waves; death was close. I spoke the battle prayer of our tuath. "Let our enemy fall into our hands. Let them stumble on their way to battle. Let their blades shatter."

Then Mael Duin called out, "Show them your weapons!" Swords and spears went up; a forest of sharp, shining blades sprang out of the black skin boat. "Come out from your hiding place and meet your death!"

It was completely still. Black smoke rose from the rocks ahead, turning in a slow column. We drifted closer and closer, our sails rippling, four lengths from the Viking boat.

There was a sudden pounding and clashing coming from behind the rocks. Mael Duin climbed up the mast to see, then swung down from the mast and his whispered words ran down the boat.

"Blacksmiths. Blacksmiths. Put down your weapons slowly and pick up your oars. Row backwards—row for your life—but don't turn around."

A breath or even a glance from a blacksmith could dull a weapon or cause it to shatter in battle. All the virtues of a weapon, its making, the runes engraved, Nuca's blessing, could be destroyed with one word from an enemy smith, who held the secrets of fire and iron.

We were still moving closer to shore, under sail. We put the oars into the water, and Mael Duin went to the helm. The Viking smiths came into view, bending over an anvil as broad as a cow's back. Our curragh shuddered and paused, then started to back against the waves. The Vikings were hidden. Minutes crept by in silence. Then suddenly a dark man appeared; he was coming down the beach fast. He had a mass of burning iron in his tongs and he hurled it straight towards us. Germane turned the boat just in time. The sea boiled around us. The second man came running with a long-hilted sword and threw it far. Turning hilt over point, it scorched a red spiral in the freezing air between us before it came down in the helm, beside Mael Duin, and stuck there. We turned and rowed out of the breakers. The Vikings screamed from the shore.

We made a wide pass of the island and the wind caught our sails again on the other side. Our boat was damaged. There was a tear in the hull as wide as three fingers. All through the dusk Brian worked with his hands in freezing water, jamming the needle through the skin from the outside of the curragh toward Germane, who stuck it back through. The rest of us bailed without stopping. Finally the level of the water began to drop, and then there was only a slow leak.

When I was a child my uncle in Achill swam to shore one night when he couldn't find a leak, but his friends drowned, and they were in warmer seas than we were. We'd been lucky; we had found the hole before the boat filled with sea and hid it. Mael Duin set a bowl of burning oil on the waves that night, as an offering, and cleaned his Viking sword. Even he was glad when dark came without another sighting of the enemy, to let a night pass between blacksmiths and a battle.

I took the first watch, and the second, letting Germane sleep through. The sky was clear and I'd never seen so many stars, or so bright. Straight over the bow, due north, a shimmering violet light moved across the sky in waves. We were still hours from dawn; the east was black. There was a distant rushing water sound off to the right, but I could see nothing but the shapes of mountainous islands along the horizon and the calm, unbroken ocean. The sound was gone when Brian awoke. I let him take the watch, and slept awhile. When I woke up the sound of falling water had come back, but it had moved to the left of the prow. I crept down the boat to Brian, climbing over bodies and weapons.

"What is it? Can you see anything?" I asked him.

"No," he whispered. "Let's go a little closer," and he

swung the tiller to the right. "Go down to the bow and look out for rocks," he told me.

I could see Mael Duin's gold hair under the mast; he was asleep. I passed him, but he didn't stir. He was curled up around the skin sack, with the hilt of the Viking sword under his hand. I got down into the prow and tied myself to the boat. As each wave went under us a phosphorescent foam appeared on the cross-hatched leather thongs binding the gunnel. The sound was in front of us now, getting louder. I kept my eyes on the water right in front of the boat, looking for ripples that might be rocks just under the surface. Brian called out, and I saw the arch of empty dark across the sky straight in front of us, where the stars disappeared. The water roared and people were waking up around me. Mael Duin grabbed the tiller from Brian and turned the curragh, so the black thing swerved over. We caught the spray when we turned and the water was warm. Someone brought a lamp into the bow. A large, brilliant salmon writhed in the air and disappeared in the dark sea below. "We have enough food," said Mael Duin, and he turned the curragh as we drew close to the rocks under the sky-stream. There was a sudden stench of rotting fish as we passed.

Mael Duin locked the steering arm, the sails filled and we swept north. He ordered everyone back to sleep, and took the watch himself. The night was half over. It was still five hours until dawn by my reckoning, but I couldn't sleep. I took my staff back to the stern and worked, cutting the ogam strokes into the wood with my father's knife. Several hours later I chipped out the marks for the sky-stream, and a sadness came on me. When I laid down my staff, Mael Duin, who hadn't spoken at all, said that I must give them the poem of the voyage. I said I would be giving it to the vultures or the whales soon enough.

"That's an unlucky thought for someone who goes into battle tomorrow," said Mael Duin, "Take it back." His eyes were narrowed, but he smiled. "Why would you think you will not survive it?"

I told him that fear would be a breach of faith, so far north.

He yanked out the steering oar and leaned on it until our prow fell under the North Star. "We're a long way from Rath Cetach, Diuran. The Vikings were like a dream then."

"And now the words I carve into my staff are hard to believe."

"The air's getting warmer." He lashed the oar to the frame, then took off his cloak.

The wind was light, with a summer warmth in it, and the sea was calm. He stood and stretched, his gold hair flying and his brown skin drinking the air. I thought: He is so alive. Something is changing us, now just when it is too late.

"The air is so clear. The stars are closer, here." He sat down beside me, twisting the rope of his skin sack in his hands. "Everything comes to a point. Tomorrow we'll see our enemy. The end is coming."

I said, "I look down the boat, and think, these would be good to die with. We've had so much. I could die right now. If I am going to die soon, let it be right now. Let it stand; I want nothing more than this."

His eyes flashed. "Then you accomplish nothing. I don't understand you."

"In the old language, before the Vikings came, the word for 'north' was 'hell'. Do you know why?" I asked him.

He put his head down in his hands, out of the wind, then looked up at the sails. "North is the place where everything becomes clear. Why did you like to sit in the highest tree on Rath Cetach? From there you could watch everything that went on below. You could be alone. The highest point in the land is the place—"

"—Where things become clear. 'On the hillside where the big stones move, where the bones live, where the bonfire is laid, where my lover falls.' "

His voice was fierce. "We have seen so much, but nothing has happened."

"But you spoke the words of the Brugh na Boinne, and brought the branch to life."

"I did nothing. It happened because you drank the sea. You wanted to die."

"Before I got the chance to go to war?"

"I saw you dead. There was nothing beyond that." His voice shook. "You would be a druid soon, if I had not asked you to come. A poet." He stopped, and then spoke again, carefully. "If there were no battle, life would have no meaning now. What has it all been for, if not for this? Once you have made a certain choice. . . going north. . . even death has meaning."

"But you made that choice when you left home. When you were fifteen."

"It wasn't the same. I wasn't thinking of anything but my name." He looked away from me, then stretched up one arm to test the oar. It was latched securely and didn't move. "It's simple. It's no good if I don't kill him." He clasped his ankles and squinted into the dark. "Up here, it seems easy."

I took his foot in my lap, and gently touched the sole with my fingers. "It's healed well; it should give you no trouble fighting tomorrow."

"We're ready."

"And you have your Viking sword."

"And you have your own father's knife." He touched the blade at my waist, then took my hand. He turned my hands over in his, saying, "Diuran of the beautiful hands. Have you slept at all tonight?"

"Little less than you."

"Lie down here." He pulled me down into his arm. "Can you stretch out? Is there room? When you look straight up, all you can see are stars. Like the chimney hole in your father's house."

"I wish we had one flask of poteen. I could get drunk. I'd give a third of my share of Viking treasure for one flask of Irish poteen."

"You could always drink instead of sleeping."

I shivered. "It's getting colder."

Mael Duin pulled his grey cloak over us and put his arms around me. We didn't move or speak for a long time. Then he said, "Look—the light is coming."

I looked into the east, where the dark was thinning out, pared down to a few strips of black cloud. In the west the stars were still sharp against the night, but in the east the sky was pale above the horizon. And there was something there; we saw it at the same moment. An island floated above the horizon. There was a flat plain with clouds and ocean below it, and the shape of a plow standing on it. We drifted across the current, and the island disappeared.

Then we saw flickering lights in the dark west and north, straight ahead, along the current. It was a ruined fortress, partially drowned. We sailed right into it. The foundations and land were completely covered by sea, but the broken walls, towers and columns loomed pale and high over us. The rath was built of a strange translucent stone. Colors distilled from the sea glowed within it; at an oar's length from a column it seemed that emeralds smouldered deep inside. The white surface was smooth but it burned, and when I pulled my hand away, it took some skin with it.

With the wind blocked the sails went slack, but the boat still moved forward on the current, as it might be carried down a river within a deep gorge. The silence was broken by occasional distant thunder as pieces of walls and towers crumbled and fell into the sea. Everyone was asleep but Mael Duin and I. The ruins went on and on, and there seemed no end to them.

Mael Duin swept the water with his hand. "Not a shred of grass, or earth. . . not even a bone. How could the sea rise, and drown the land?"

"The moon makes tides everyday—"

"—Here, with the moon and sea so close, she must be powerful."

There was a fluttering near the top of a wall. As we came around it and looked back, a large white owl shifted in his hole. The stars were fading above us, but the moon was still bright when she appeared behind the ruins. Shadows were growing under the towers, between them, shafts of gold light.

"Calibrators," I said, pointing to the towers, "maybe they're calibrators. Like the standing stones at Brugh na Boinne or Carrowmore—made to measure the length of days and the phases of the moon."

He picked up a rowing oar, and pushed us off a white chunk of column that was sticking up like a deadhead in the middle of the dark water. He spoke from the song of making. " 'Who shapes weapons from hill to hill?' "

I told him that Nuca had taken me into the hill, at the Brugh na Boinne, and showed me where, more than a thousand years ago, they forged metals in the stone basins and hammered bronze along the beam of light shaped by the passageway at the winter solstice. Nuca said those were the swords that never broke or bent in battle.

"They were farmers who kept the land before us, and they had such magic," he said. There was anguish in his voice. "Diuran... we have never fought together. How will I find you?"

We made a plan. If either of us got in trouble we would call out "Fylgja!," the Viking word for ghost. Maybe it would give us a moment—in their confusion—to find each other.

When we came out into the open sea again, the sun was just coming up. Behind us the rath came alive, flashing brilliant light, then dimmed as the fog began to rise. The crew woke up, and there was food to prepare and weapons to make ready.

8

We sailed that morning into a cloud. The fog had seemed light and patchy, but we had not gone three lengths into it when the cloud closed up overhead. Mael Duin kept the tiller bar rigid, and Germane, beside me, closed his eyes. Our weapons looked cold and tired under the mist. Then we got our first sign that day of the Vikings.

A woman was crying somewhere close by. It wasn't the keening, but furious screaming, and her curses were Irish. Mael Duin leaned on the tiller, the boat swung out, and we rowed hard towards the sound. Now we could hear breakers, too; land was somewhere near. We broke out of the cloud. There was a boat before us, the stern deck covered in flames and smoke.

Under the forward mast a tall, black-haired woman screamed into the mist. She held a naked young girl under the arms. The girl's hair touched the deck and covered the end of the rope that was wound taut around her neck. Above her head, from the mast, dangled a piece of hemp. Mael Duin called out, and the dark woman turned and saw us.

"Look! Look what you've done! Are you proud heroes?"

She had a long knife in her hand and she laid the blade against her own neck. "Keep back, Viking bastards—or you can watch me die with my curse on you, and none of you will get pleasure from a woman for the rest of your lives. Your little power will feel the thrust of my knife inside you, if you ever take a woman....Let the pain drive you to your death if you ever take a woman against her will."

"Your boat is on fire—do you want to be burned alive?" cried Mael Duin.

It was a mistake. At that moment she knew we were Irish. If it was a trap, then he'd laid us bare for the slaughter. She dropped the knife and went down on her knees. Lifting the dead girl in her arms, she kissed the pale face and cradled it in her neck and rocked her. She didn't weep.

Mael Duin steered us towards the long boat. She laid the girl gently down and stripped off her own dress. Her body was spare and muscular, her shoulders broad like a boy's, but her breasts were full. She covered the dead girl, then took fire from the stern with a broken oar and caught the mainsail and the foresail. Our prow nearly touched hers. Mael Duin was getting ready to leap onto the deck when she dove into the sea.

"Trial by drowning," said Germane. "She was innocent—no Viking." But in a moment she came up some distance from the boat and swam with strong strokes towards the shore. She ran up the rocky bank and disappeared.

We had trouble getting our boat in through the rocks and breakers to the beach, but when we pulled up on the sand, the woman, covered in a long cloak, came riding down the beach on a grey horse. She passed us with our weapons drawn and stopped, watching the boat as the flames devoured it. We kept an eye on the rocks above us, but nothing came over them.

When the mast fell and the flames died out, she rode down to us. She stopped before Mael Duin and got off her horse.

"What is this island?" I asked, moving forward with my hand on the hilt of my sword.

"My home, poet." Her voice was deep, rough now

with smoke and sorrow. Her eyes were strange, foreign; her dark red mouth was beautiful, cut in a perfect shape. "Put your sword away. There are no Vikings here. I am Epona of Cua, the tuath that settled the Arans and the western isles, queen of this island." She turned to Mael Duin. "You are chieftain?"

"We heard you," said Mael Duin, "a long way in the fog. But we saw only one boat."

"That was mine. The Vikings burnt it, so we could not escape. When they come back, they don't want to look for us all over the northern sea." She was tall. She looked over his shoulder while she talked, and it seemed as though all her will was driven against the desire to run. She had the cornered look of someone who is unused to company, like an animal or a hermit—but I could see the power in her, something she kept back out of policy. If she ran it would be very fast, and not entirely out of fear, but also out of wildness. I could imagine her watching, judging us from a shadowed corner of a shrine, better than greeting chieftains—still, she was a queen, and she could talk to anybody.

"Kinsman, I couldn't see the shape of your boat in the mist. She was my daughter, she was twelve years old today. The man who raped her had red hair and a red beard; there is no such man among you. His name is Torvald—he has a fort beyond the Blasket Islands, off an Daingin."

Mael Duin gasped. "Where is he?"

"Gone, for now, but knowing there are women here, he will be back. I must go."

"I thought today would be his last. We—" he began.

"Wait—" I grabbed his arm, to warn him to silence, but she cut him off before he could finish.

"I would find him and kill him today, if it were not for

my daughters. I can't leave them alone without protection."

"He is my enemy. He is the man we've been hunting for a year. I am Mael Duin of the Eoganacht."

She took his hand, not gently, but as a man does to a man, and looked at him. "You won't be able to track him now, in this fog." She looked over his shoulder at the black, spiraling smoke. "Will you wait here for one hour and watch?"

He turned to us. "Diuran, you're in charge; watch the beach. Germane, come with me—"

"Please don't come farther until I return. I haven't told her sisters yet. If you would watch for me, Mael Duin." Then she said quickly, "In the name of the goddess," and dropped his hand. He held the reins as she climbed up on the horse. She dug her bare heels into his side; the long knife at her waist flashed as she rode up the sand.

"You let her go. In one hour we'll be dead, if she needs that much time to warn her 'daughters'," said Germane. "She's no Irish woman. Did you hear the way she talked, Diuran? And she called you poet!"

I spit on the sand. "She looks like a witch."

"Maybe she's from Achill, or a tribe in the east, from Kildare or beyond," said Brian.

"She speaks carefully," I said.

Germane said, "Her voice is deep for a woman."

"You can't doubt she's a woman, though, Viking or witch," said Brian, laughing. "But she's younger than me; twenty-three or -four, at the most. That wasn't her daughter, who hung herself on the ship. There, she's lying."

Mael Duin said sharply, "I don't know you at all. We have the same enemy; her shame is our shame. You should cut his tongue who says a word against her." Then he walked away from us, down to the water. While he stood there, his back straight and still in the moment before he bent down, I knew he would pick up a stone and throw it, and I thought to myself, if he does, we are doomed, he is half in love with her already.

We watched the beach and the cliffs behind us. The fog moved back past the breakers but did not lift. We saw no other ships or Vikings at all that day, and the queen sent us food, with a plea that we might watch the beach for three days, so she could mourn her child in peace. Germane said that was adequate time to gather enough Viking longboats to fill the northern sea. We made a camp on the beach, and kept our weapons polished, watching the fog for a Viking prow. The mist remained, and the yellow gorse began to fade and die. We decided to risk bringing the curragh farther up the beach. We turned her over and scraped the hull, and rubbed her down with pig grease.

Mael Duin collected the blackened bones that washed in with wood and seaweed. He buried them under a small cairn of smooth stones near the water, and he put the skull of his father into the mound. When he put the last stone on top and walked away, a red-mouthed black cormorant perched there, and soon another joined him. All day long they stretched their wings and screeched. We tossed them scraps of roasted fish, which they devoured and then began to scream again.

On the evening of the third day she rode down to us. Her horse was groomed and dressed in silver, and she herself wore the helmet and weapons of a warrior queen. She rode straight down to Mael Duin, got off her horse, and put the reins in his hand.

"I have a banquet prepared for you. Will you come to my house and rest now?"

"The sea is rough enough tonight, with autumn coming, but we shouldn't leave the beach unguarded."

"We will not. Bring your weapons," she said. Mael Duin went down the beach to his camp and strapped the Viking sword to his waist.

She turned to Brian and said in a low voice, "What is your name?"

"Brian of Cashel."

"Brian, if three of you will stay here to watch, I will send meat and drink. My maidservants have been here for ten years. They have been virgins too long, don't you think?"

"Perhaps. How old are these maids?" laughed Brian.

"Old enough to have dreams, and young enough for you," she smiled, her eyes narrowing. "Will you stay?"

"Yes. But when will you send these women?"

"When Mael Duin sits at my table," she said.

So Brian and two others stayed behind on the beach while the rest of us, bearing arms, followed Mael Duin and the queen.

Her large house was whitewashed like a cottage. She led us to a long low table in the middle of the banquet hall where there were large cushions to sit on, and pewter cups and plates of food at each place. The hall had high, dark-beamed ceilings; the two long walls were hung with brilliant blue silk. At the farthest, narrowest end of the room hung a tapestry of the pale floating rath that we had sailed through several days before. Opposite was the hearth, and beside it a wide doorway which opened into the entranceway, and then a courtyard with a dark pond surrounded by stone benches.

She put her sword and helmet on the table. Both were worked with gold filigree and set with amber and lapis. "Let us share weapons," she said. "What do men of Erin

carry now, that roam the north seas? Show me!" Several
men unstrapped their spears or knives and laid them in
the center of the table. Two dark-haired girls poured red
wine from skin sacks into our cups, then waited by the
door for Epona's sign. She waved to them, and they set
the sacks carefully down.

"We'll serve ourselves now. My daughters must go to
bed." She rose and kissed them each, then walked a ways
out of the room with them. She came back with three
women dressed in warm cloaks and scarves, all but their
eyes and their bright cheeks hidden. Epona talked to
them, and I heard her say, "Fedlimid, do only what you
like." They laughed. "You have something?" asked
Epona. The woman showed her a long knife, stuck in a
belt under her cloak. "All of you? Fine." Then Epona
strung a wine sack over each girl's shoulder and sent
them out.

She had given Mael Duin the place of honor, the head
of the table, with his back to the fire. I sat on his left,
Germane sat across from me. She stood behind Mael
Duin, and filled his glass from a red crystal flask, which
she took from a small table behind her. As she poured,
she saw me watching her. She asked, "Why haven't you
brought your ollamh staff, Diuran? We have no druid in
this house; I'd like to hear your poems."

"Why do you think I am a poet?"

She looked around the table, at all the men, wondering. "It's obvious, isn't it? You've been a sailor for one
year, but there are still signs of the ollamh about you.
Now that you're in my house, you may be free. You must
call me Epona. I can't read the ogam language, but I
know a poet's manners." She laughed. "Well, I have
known many. I am a queen." Her eyes narrowed and her
voice became serious. "And I recognize your eyes, your

194

healing hands, and the love he bears you." She looked down at Mael Duin, with his forehead damp under his gold hair and the fire behind him. She put her hand on his shoulder.

"Epona, what is that place in the tapestry?" I asked.

"Didn't you see it, south of this island?"

"Yes, but what is it? There are no songs about it."

"I know nothing about that place, but the Vikings call it the Elk's Gallows. Perhaps you will make a poem about it. May I see your sword, Mael Duin?" He turned the hilt and laid it on the table.

"That's no Irish weapon," she said.

"No, a Viking blacksmith threw it at me."

"You must tell me sometime how you managed to survive that. But this is a beautiful blade." She turned it over and looked at it as if she were deciphering some message. "Do you see these lines, like waves?"

"Like a field of corn—"

"Yes, exactly. They are called the bloovarp, like the vertical threads on a loom. When these lines meet the veins of blood or the guts of a man or woman, then the weaving is complete." She threaded the fingers of both hands and shoved them together. "Do you understand?"

"Yes. Excuse me. I'm not used to the warmth; I'll be back in a minute." He got up from the table and went out toward the courtyard.

Epona picked up Mael Duin's glass, circled the rim with her finger, then finished it. She leaned over to Germane and touched the blade. She said, "He forgot his sword," and began to laugh. She threaded her hands again, making the gesture with her hands that means sex. She laughed, and Germane laughed, too. We were all drunk, but she filled our cups again from the wine-skin, and wiped their edges with a fine piece of silk.

"I imagine that you're a very good lover, Germane. You probably had your first woman when you were about fourteen years old."

Germane laughed nervously and leaned in. "Thirteen."

"I knew it. You seem so sure of yourself, so sensitive. Very experienced. I'll bet there isn't much you haven't tried." He drained his glass. His face was red. "Your brother thinks I'm a witch. Do you?" His eyebrows went up.

"Diuran sees things that other people don't see, doesn't he? He has a gift. But he's worried because sometimes he can't tell the difference between his own fears and real danger." She turned the sword over. "I'm not going to hurt anyone. I never asked the Vikings to come here; all I want is peace."

She stopped and looked up. Mael Duin was standing in the door. She stood and her sleeveless robe of silver mesh fell from her hips, and kept falling down, like a fine mist of rain. She picked up the Viking sword. Her bare arms were strong and the muscles flexed as she swung the weapon slightly. I stood up, and Mael Duin put his arm around her and laughed, saying, "You can't come with me, Diuran."

When I woke up the candles on the table were guttering, and everyone was asleep. It was dark outside. There was just enough light on the table to see the weapons among the wine jars and the crusts of bread. Germane had his cloak over his head, curled up on the cushion. I got up quietly and walked out into the hall. I had no idea where Mael Duin had gone. The candles in the wall sconces were burned out. I passed three doors that led to empty rooms, then the fourth was locked. There was a small window at the top of the door, and within I could see Epona's daughters sleeping. The last door on the right, partly opened, was in a little alcove. When I walked up to it a low growl came out of the dark. A huge wolfhound lay before the threshold. I stepped back, and the dog rose. Then he turned and went into the room. He lay down at the foot of the bed and watched me.

Mael Duin was lying on his side, his back to the door, watching her sleep. Epona was curled inside the arch of his body. Her head was bent, her legs tucked up, one arm folded with the hand flat against his bare chest. Her mass of hair was spread across the sheet behind her, and her face was turned towards him. He was whispering something, not to her; it sounded like a prayer. The dog raised its head and looked at him. Then he covered her hand with his own. Epona's lips parted and moved, silently, her eyes still closed. Then she said, "Mael Duin" and put her arm around his neck. They folded into each other and I went away.

Every night after that Mael Duin stayed with her in a small tower at the point of the island. The sea washed one side of the tower; at the first level a hook in the stone moored a small curragh. A shallow stairway led up through three thick oak floors with swinging trapdoors. There was a hearth at each level, and small arched windows through which the wind always blew. They had a view of the breakers halfway around the island. Some small cliff birds had a nest at the peak of the roof.

Throughout that autumn and winter, Epona left Mael Duin each day at dawn and rode to the fort at the other end of the island. The tuath came to her to settle disputes, to ask for help or just to talk, she said. She let neither Mael Duin nor anyone else of our crew come with her, but we didn't complain. The rest of the island was ours to hunt, or practice archery, or ride, or sleep all day if we wanted to. We slept on the cushions around the table in the hall. Germane spent most of each day with a dark-haired girl with green eyes, and most of us found someone to keep company with, too.

Mael Duin looked after the horses each morning. There were seventy in Epona's limestone stables—horses much bigger than we had in Erin, with long, arched necks and elegant heads. Most were grey with spotted rumps, but there were a few all white and one or two dark roans. Epona never seemed to favor one over another, but would ride any easily—stallion, gelding or mare— across the island each day. She and Mael Duin were well matched as riders. At Samhain Epona held races all day long, on the beach, and across the island.

One morning I walked to the stable to see if Mael Duin wanted to go for a ride, but I couldn't find him. A horse came in by himself with no rider, wet with foam and breathing hard. I cooled him down and gave him some water, then went to the house. A woman in a brown cloak was just turning at the end of the hallway; I could see her black hair coming out of her cloak. I called Epona, but she didn't hear me. I turned the corner, and she was gone. That night at dinner I teased her and asked why she didn't speak to me, and she seemed surprised. She had not left the judgment hall all day, but had only gotten back a few moments ago. Mael Duin said he himself had been walking, looking for her, because she was late.

One morning after that—it was the day before the winter solstice—it was raining hard and I found myself in the empty dining hall. The windows high above the doorway faced east, and the room was flooded with soft grey light. I stood beneath the tapestry at the other end of the room. Now I saw what I had missed in candlelight.

It was much more than just an image of the floating ruins. It was a map of the northern and western sea. By my calculations it seemed that if we cut south and east across the current, stopping at one large island for water, we should reach Erin in twenty days or less. Mael Duin came into the room, and I showed him what I had found. He said, "But why should we leave? We have everything we need here." Then he touched the weaving and said, "Her work is wonderful, isn't it? I've never seen weaving like this before, have you?"

That night as we ate together in the hall, Epona stretched across Mael Duin's cushion as he said, "Diuran tells me that in twenty days we could reach Erin."

"I'd like to sail with Diuran the Navigator," she said. "I imagine he has fine stories of his travels—but he won't tell them to me."

"Why don't you ask Mael Duin?" I said.

She laughed and threaded her arms around his neck. "Is it good for lovers to know too much about each other? I don't like to be inquisitive."

"Not ever?" asked Brian.

She closed her eyes. "Well...except, I want to know everything about my enemy...." She looked at Mael Duin and smiled, "and the less he knows about me the better."

"Mystery commands respect," said Brian.

Then Mael Duin asked her if she would come with us to Erin.

"Of course," she replied, kissing him, "I'd love that, but how will I tell my children that I'm deserting them? Never mind," she laughed, "I'll think of something. But let's sail to the moon instead in your great curragh."

He smoothed her hair and laughed. "Then we'd better go tomorrow night; it's the longest night of the year."

"It's not as far as it seems."

"You've been there before?"

"Many times."

"Did you go alone?"

"Sometimes."

"Who went with you?"

"A piper. A harpist, several poets. But I've never been with a great traveler like Mael Duin."

"When the Viking is dead, we'll go," he said.

The next afternoon Germane and I left Mael Duin on the ridge above the beach, tying off straw bundles for the bonfire. We went up to the house together. I said to him, "He hasn't told her anything about the voyage."

"Maybe he's protecting her. But I think there's some other reason." At that moment we were passing the three locked rooms and I heard something. I motioned to Germane to keep quiet. Someone was inside—a woman, singing in a strange language. Germane brought his sword out, and I kicked the middle door. "Who's there?"

The door opened slowly. Epona looked out. She saw our weapons and asked what was wrong.

"What are you doing here?" I asked her.

"Looking for something. You can't help, Diuran," she said, smiling. "You don't know what it is."

"What's in there?"

There was nothing, she told us, only thread, wool, and old things that belonged to her daughters. "No weapons or instruments of torture," she said.

I told her that I'd seen her ride off that morning.

She looked sideways at me. "Are you sure of that?"

"Why are you keeping us here?"

"Keeping you? I hadn't really thought of it that way."

"You're Viking, aren't you?"

She looked at the ground for a moment, then her eyes fastened on mine and she smiled. "Yes, of course. You're right, Diuran, you do have the sight; you see everything. You have such a gift. You shouldn't waste it."

"Does Mael Duin know this?"

She looked at me in wonder. "Of course. Did you think I wouldn't tell him that? If you don't believe me, ask him. Or if you're too ashamed, I'll tell you myself. I don't mind. My mother was an Irish queen, my father a Viking raider. She was not willing. But he kept us and I can speak the Viking tongue. You heard the song, just now. My daughters don't know the language. Their father was pure Irish. Do you want to come in?"

"No," said Germane. His face was red. "Let's go, Diuran."

The night was clear and dry, and the bonfire burned fast. Mael Duin led Epona's cattle and horses through the embers, as our father had always done on Lough Corrib, then raked the ash aside and covered it to keep for the spring planting. We all went into the dining hall afterwards to drink poteen and eat meat. Epona finally joined us, taking her place on Mael Duin's right. Her eyes were brilliant and her cheeks red from the cold. She wore a long, loosely woven cape of emerald green and violet wool over her silver dress. It was fastened with a heavy silver brooch.

Mael Duin stood behind her. Gently, he drew the pin out of the brooch, lifted the shawl from her shoulders and put it over his arm. Then he suddenly froze, staring at the brooch in his hand. He turned Epona around to face him.

"Where did you get this?" Everyone got up from the table.

"I. . . I don't remember," she answered. She pulled her arm away gently; he grasped it harder.

"Try."

"I don't know, Mael Duin. I have so many jewels. What's wrong with you?"

"You have so many; she had only one. You got it from the wife of Ailill Ocar Aga. You are his murderer."

"I don't know what you're talking about. I've never heard of him. Who is he? A kinsman of yours?"

"Yes, Epona, my love. He was my father. He gave this brooch to my mother before I was born."

"Let go of me, Mael Duin." Her voice had an edge now to match his, but colder. She twisted her arm and stepped away. "Mael Duin, you would rather kill me now than listen to a word I have to say. Maybe I would rather die than tell you the truth. Brian, take my children out of here." When they were gone, she said, with a harsh laugh, "It seems that this love between us is uneven."

"Love? There has been nothing but treachery between us!"

"Yes, I see that, but not the way you mean. There is no blood between us, Mael Duin. I've never seen this man, your father. The other, the Viking—I had no choice. I had to give him hospitality, you understand, to protect my daughters. He promised not to touch them—he promised to leave as soon as his boat was mended. But then that morning. . . I saw the sails go up, and they raped my daughter on their ship. The captain, the one with the red hair, I killed."

"What!"

"Shall I tell you how? He came back to say goodbye; I embraced him at the doorway of this house and stabbed him through the throat. Oh, there was blood all over the step. It took twelve sacks of lime to get it out. I had hidden my poor, frightened child in the tower; when I went back there she was gone. I ran down to the beach and found her hanging from the mast of my own boat. She'd killed herself. They set fire to the boat and sailed away.

"I picked up the brooch afterwards. It was on his cloak. That's what I had for my girl's life. It belonged to her. I wore it for her, tonight, because it was the feast. I'm not sorry for any of it. I dream of killing the rest of them, night after night, in different ways.

"Now Mael Duin, I will confess to you, in front of all these friends: I didn't tell you this because I was afraid you would leave me. Now you see my weakness. Now be angry."

"Angry? Hardly. I am in your debt; you have killed my enemy."

"I don't want you in my debt; I despise any affection you give me out of obligation. I don't want you to stay here because of that. I don't need your protection. In fact," she said, "I'm much stronger alone. We shared an enemy; that's all. You were practical. I was the bait for the trap. You were only waiting for him. You never loved me at all, I see that. Get out."

He looked at her a long time and then turned to the rest of us, his face hard, and said, "We'll leave for home at the first break in the weather. We'll camp on the beach until then."

She picked up her cloak and left the room. The next day she sent packages of dried meat, roots, oatmeal and water skins by messengers but never came to the beach herself. The sky was clear. We packed the curragh that night, and I walked with Mael Duin to the tower to get his sword. There was a light coming from the highest window. His sword was stuck in the sand beside the door. As we walked away, her voice came down, in a clear chant.

"Tonight my hands are old. The wick dries up. What do I care if out in the dark the sailors drown?"

I spit in the sand to keep the curse off, but Mael Duin said it didn't mean anything. When we got back to camp it was pitch black. The moon hadn't risen yet, and the tower was hidden by the cliff. We had wrapped ourselves in sheepskins by the fire when something began to happen in the sky, in the direction of the tower. At first I thought it was a falling star, but then the streak of light came again and did not dissolve like the path of a star. Another and another came until soon there were too many to count. Narrow, colored beams of light stretched across the sky, quivering, like silk threads held taut.

Mael Duin walked down to the water, watching the sky, but the others were afraid. "Is the witch doing that?" Germane asked, and Brian said it was a good thing we were going home. The lights began to cross and weave. I got up and went down to Mael Duin.

"She has comfort in this," he said.

"Everyone will be glad to get home. We all need comfort; we're tired." The beams began to diminish. I said, "This island is beautiful, but there's no rest, no peace here."

"There was."

"It was false. Your father's spirit is avenged. There is true comfort."

"I don't feel it."

"You will. You can go home."

"You don't need to watch me, Diuran. My despair has been your burden long enough. Soon I'll feel nothing. She's right—you'll be a poet and a healer—some chieftain will treasure you for it. Let's go back to camp; it's our last chance to stretch out on solid ground."

There was a strong shore breeze blowing the next morning, but the sky was clear and the breakers low and even. We rowed easily out of the foam, Mael Duin at the helm. Germane and I rigged the sails and we began to slide along the shore. When we passed the point, we would raise the mainsail and be free of the island.

We approached the tower, where the turquoise shallows dropped off into the purple deep water. The wind picked up. Suddenly Epona appeared on the beach. Her long hair and her cloak were blowing out behind her. There was a loop of yarn in her hand. When our boat passed, she swung her arm as if she were getting ready to throw a javelin, then let go. The strand soared over the water and Mael Duin let go of the steering paddle and caught the end in his hand.

Then Brian screamed, "We can't get out of the riptide!" We were being pulled into the rocks. Germane frantically tried to unwind the mast ropes. The mast was going to snap any moment. We were going sideways into the breakers; the waves were exploding over us. Mael Duin leaned on the tiller, and the boat swerved around. There was a deep shudder as we hit the sand. The boat was half-swamped, but the wind was so bad, with sand and spray flying, we couldn't see if the hull was torn. Epona ran up to us, breathless. "I saw it coming from the tower—the tide was coming in sideways all morning. You'll have to tie her down quickly. It's going to get worse."

Mael Duin screamed his orders and we moved fast until the boat was moored high on the beach and our weapons were safe. Then I caught up with Germane and Brian, who were waiting for me, and we followed Mael

Duin, with his arm around Epona, up the rocks to the house. Mael Duin said that we would stay until spring.

From that night I turned against him. She had enchanted him, but he had betrayed us. I couldn't live in her house, so I left them and built a clochan on the mountain. There were stones scattered from some ancient, ruined cairn, but there was nothing in the memory of the people of the island or feeling in the place itself to tell what they had been. They fit together well, and my shelter was built quickly. I made an entrance facing the sea and a window on the back wall. The roof was low and corbeled. I couldn't stand up in it, but the clochan was long enough to stretch out and sleep in.

I cooked my fish beside the river, under the bank where the wind was mild. There was always wind on top of the mountain. Sometimes it was impossible to stand. When I got caught cutting turf, or fishing in the river halfway down the mountain, then I had to crawl to the clochan over heather that was laid flat by the gale. Storms moved in fast, sometimes with heavy rain and hail, but I was rarely surprised because the sky was immense and I could see everything. I ate what I could find on the mountain: hazelnuts, berries, and roots, trout and watercress from the river. From the mountain I could see the ocean change color with the sky, and sometimes see the waves breaking white when no boat would be going out. But I couldn't hear the sea, and that suited me, too.

There were no other dwellings on that side of the island except some rough booleys beside the crich—the corn ridges—and the shearing huts that no one used anymore. It was hard at first, being alone. Even though Nuca could go for a day or more without speaking, his vigilance had been company. And after one year in the curragh, it was strange to have room around me. But the hunger for company lessened. The birds began to get used to me; one morning I woke and a kestrel was sitting on the broad sill of my window. Still, at odd times, when I wasn't thinking of him at all, suddenly Mael Duin was vivid before me, as he had been on the last part of our voyage through the floating rath, or in childhood.

The voyage itself began to subside. I cut myself a diamond willow wand for a walking stick and put the ogam yew staff away. Fragments of songs and poems became jumbled in my head. Part of a poem would keep me awake, running over and over, and then stick on to some other verse that had nothing to do with it. Sometimes it went on until the sound of the words made them meaningless. And sometimes I'd go out of the clochan and sit in the dark, facing the wind, and it would stop after awhile.

I watched the clouds or the long grass swept by waves of wind, and I knew that I needed nothing else. Spring and summer passed, autumn came, and I saw the changes of birds and weeds. The curragh remained tethered below. The sun moved toward the equinox. I watched the shadows change inside my clochan, and when Germane came up the mountain to show me his child, I gave him the greeting that we say in the days before Samhain, and he knew that I had not lost track of time.

I held his son of six months with his fat fists and light hair, wrapped in a woven blanket. Then he took the baby and gave it to his wife, who stayed back behind the clochan.

"Will you come down to us for Samhain?" he asked me.

I said no, and asked about Mael Duin.

"I don't live in her house anymore myself, but whenever I see them, they seem very well together. They sleep in the tower beside the water. Brian is still at the house and Epona talks to him." I looked at Germane, but he said nothing else.

"Is she loyal to Mael Duin?"

"She talks rough, she'll say anything, but not in front of Mael Duin—and never a word against him. Brian told me that she came to the island ten years ago, and that after her husband died she burned their boat so that she'd have no choice but to stay, and keep his promise to protect the people. Every day she goes to the keep on the south shore."

"You see her?" I asked.

"She rides past our cottage in the morning."

"Who else is still at her house?"

"Only Brian, I think. He sleeps with one of her kitchen maids, the one that Epona sent that first night to him." Then he said that Epona wanted to have another child. She wanted me to come down, to give her some mixture, out of my knowledge, to help her conceive.

I asked Germane if he wanted to go home. No, he said, his only fear was that he might lose what he had, if there was something between Epona and Brian—if Mael Duin found out. I told him that I would come down in two days, with herbs and roots for Epona, but that she must live apart from Mael Duin for one week before Samhain.

So Epona moved back into the house, and Mael Duin stayed in the tower, and I slept in the cottage with my brother's small family.

Mael Duin leaned over the half door the first morning, looking at me. "Thank you for coming," he said.

I shook the sleep out. I hadn't rested well my first night off the mountain.

"No trouble," I said. Everyone else was gone.

"The sun's been up for two hours, by the dial in the yard," he said, swinging the door in. "Epona's left."

"I'll come outside." I brushed the thatch off my cloak and went out into the yard. Germane's wife was drawing water from the well and the baby, lying on his back on a thick rug, was watching his feet move against the sky. Mael Duin stooped down by him and said, "Come here, little bear," and picked him up. The woman turned around, smiling, then went back to her work. Mael Duin was no longer gaunt. His shoulders and chest were broader, his face with his golden hood had the look of a gyrfalcon.

"You want a child of your own, Mael Duin?"

"You said that just like Nuca. I've missed you, Diuran. There's more of the druid about you since you've been on the mountain," he said.

"No, you're wrong. There's less. I put the staff away."

"I've put the voyage behind me, too. It's like a dream now."

"Do you tell Epona your dreams?"

"No," he replied, looking surprised. "Why?"

"I wouldn't share those memories with a woman who would bear my child," I said quietly.

"I've told her nothing of the voyage. She knows nothing about it."

"I'm glad," I told him. "You've changed, Mael Duin. And there's no reason why the madness should be passed on."

"What are you saying?"

"Nothing. Are you afraid you might still be mad? That's ended, hasn't it?"

"Why do you say that to me? What do you see,

Diuran? If I thought that...if it came back, I would kill myself before I let her see it, before we had a child."

"Be quiet, Mael Duin," I said, looking at Germane's wife. Her back was still to us. "Do you want everyone to hear? Why are you so upset? If Epona's not past the time of bearing then you should have a healthy child. We won't discuss it."

Every morning when Epona rode past the cottage she stopped and drank a tea from linden flower and yarrow root and other things that I made for her. She was remote and respectful, with the same reticence that I'd seen in her the first morning that we'd come to the island.

I set a guard on the curragh and sent Germane to watch the stables from the time Epona rode past until dusk. Late one morning, Germane came panting in through the door to the cottage, saying, "The horse has come back in by himself."

"Where's Mael Duin?"

"His mare is tied up by the tower."

"Good. Did you see Brian?"

"No, I went into the dining hall—his sword was hanging on the wall, but he wasn't there. The kitchen is deserted, and her daughters are down on the strand."

"Let's go."

"What are you going to do?"

"Nothing," I said, taking my sword and the yew staff. "I'm going to look in a room."

The house was very still. A light breeze from the open door lifted the petals in a bowl of wild roses. Several of these drifted down to the table, swirled as if on water, and stopped. Two wide bands of light crossed the tapestry, dulling the image of the rath. We walked down the hall. The second door beyond her daughters' room was unlatched. I gripped the hilt of my sword and pushed the door open.

It was very dark inside, except for the light coming down from a small window across the room. Flecks of dust circulated in the wide beam. The white birch floor was bare, and there was no bed, not even a single cushion. The room was almost empty except for a huge tapestry fixed to the standing loom that ran the length of the wall.

The first thing I saw was the curragh next to the Viking island. It rode high on a wave, in a tremendous storm. The weaving was so realistic that it seemed as if I could walk into it. To the right of that was a rock covered with long-necked birds, and then a rock with a beast—half horse and half dog—snarling at the boat. The voyage was complete. The curragh was covered with giant ants, and then it sailed free under a full moon. At the top of the mast an eagle had a woman in its beak, and below, one man held another in his arms. Giant horses rose out of the sea, and then the foaming waves turned into silver spirals. There was the cave, full of sleeping men. The apple tree at the center of the tapestry was immense; its branches spread out ten times the length of the curragh.

But there was more before the voyage. At the beginning—the far left edge of the weaving—there was an image of a church, and a young woman with a Brigid's cross in her open hand lay under a man with an eagle's head. In the next image the same man, with a red hole in his chest, was inside a burning chapel. Outside the church a red-haired Viking stood beside a black-haired woman who held a dripping dagger in one hand, and a silver brooch in the other. Then there was a lake, and a woman holding a baby, and after that Mael Duin as a young man, casting a stone on Rath Cetach.

On the far right—the last scene—the curragh was on
fire, and Epona, in her silver robe, with the Viking sword
in her hand, knelt over the body of Mael Duin. The
weaving was unfinished.

The door behind us slammed. She must have been
standing there, watching us look at the cloth the whole
time.

Running out into the hall with our swords drawn, we
saw no one at either end. We went back into the room.
Germane began to scream, "It's happening again. It's the
same thing, again. We've got to get to the boat. How are
we going to find everyone?"

"Go ring the alarm bell, outside by the well." Then at
that moment Mael Duin came into the room. His Viking
sword was in his hand.

"What's wrong?" he asked.

"We sail now. Get everyone together quickly—down to
the beach," I said to Germane.

"What's wrong with you?" Mael Duin demanded.
Germane ran out past him.

"Look."

He walked to the loom. "What is this?"

"It's Epona's work. This is where she's spent her days,
Mael Duin. Everything's been a lie from the beginning."

"Where is she?"

"Are you mad? Don't you understand? Look! She
killed your father, she's going to kill you. She's Viking.
She's the enemy!"

"I have to see her. What have you done—"

"Don't you know who she is? Viking! Witch! Mate of
the red-bearded Viking who's bragged of his wife's kill for
twenty years. I don't know where she is, but everything
that's happened has been because she made it. Everything she's said has been a lie. Except one thing—she's

barren—I believe that—and who was that girl she sacrificed to get your sympathy? She set fire to the boat herself; she's done it before!"

"You don't know—this is no proof—you could be making a mistake, Diuran. We've run away too quickly in the past—"

"She's a killer."

"I never knew my father—"

"Mael Duin, don't say it. You shame yourself—"

"How many Vikings did he kill? How many women, how many children?"

"Vikings? He was a raider—My god, you're sick! You don't even know what you're saying—when we get away from here, it'll be different—Mael Duin, look at the last panel. Look how she plans to kill you—"

"She's given me everything. I'm not afraid of her. I love her." The floor was lurching. I thought I was going to be sick. Mael Duin was standing there, looking at me. Outside I could hear Germane, screaming, and the bell ringing loud.

"Listen to Germane. He's terrified out of his skull." I grabbed him by the shoulders. "This is the battle, Mael Duin. This is it—and I pray that I may get the chance to destroy the enemy. The crew is waiting. You must get control of yourself. I'm going to them now, Mael Duin, and you have to come with me." I turned away from him and ripped the tapestry with my sword. When it hung in shreds on the frame I left the room.

Epona stood in the door to the courtyard. The pool was still and green behind her. I stepped aside to let Mael Duin go forward, my hand on the hilt of my sword. He came up beside me, his face grave. There was a shred of silver mesh in his left hand, the Viking sword in the other. He stood still, looking at her.

I said, "Here is your enemy, Mael Duin. There are no secrets left. She knows everything about you. You have a weapon, Mael Duin. Kill her."

Epona put her arms around him. She said, "Oh my love, stay with me. If you stay with me you will never grow old, you will never die. Everything you need will be given to you." He didn't move or raise his arms from his side. She turned her head, laying her cheek on his shoulder, and closed her eyes. They stood together without moving. The bell stopped.

I said, "I'm going now, Mael Duin." He moved out of her embrace, put the hilt of the Viking sword in her hand, and walked with me out of the house. When we got down to the beach, Germane was surrounded, telling what he had seen. The rest of the crew were dragging the curragh down to the water.

We were past the breakers, putting up the sail, when she rode down to the sand. She cried out, "Mael Duin!" and flung out the silver rope. For a second it hung above us like a comet's tail, then it came down in the stern. Brian, who was standing next to Mael Duin at the tiller, caught the end. I could feel the boat shudder and the drag of the riptide under us. I pulled my sword from my belt, swung it, and cut off Brian's hand at the wrist. The boat slipped free and the wind picked up the sails. The tiller swung out and we were headed southeast toward home.

9

By my calculations it was four days to the next island. We gave Brian as much poteen as he could drink, then I tied off the veins with flax and sewed his wrist to his side, as I had seen Nuca do once, so the flesh would grow together without rotting. We had clear skies and Mael Duin steered by the stars and sun. I worked on my ogam staff.

On the second day out the ocean was as still as a mirror, with only a ripple in it trailing from our curragh, and the perfect reflection of everything overhead: a stray white cloud, a bird, our sails. The next day we saw the shadow of the hull and the rigging running along the white sand under us. The bottom looked so close it seemed possible to touch it by leaning over the side, although we were in deep ocean. A hundred brilliant orange and yellow fish would break suddenly out of the tall green foliage. The undersea trees moved slowly and constantly, as though there was a great wind under the water. Just before sunset, Brian, who lay with his cheek on the gunnel, saw a dragon curled around a thick green trunk. But the curragh was moving so fast that by the time Germane had grabbed his long spear, the beast was behind us, and there was only sand with undulating purple flowers below.

The next day, the feast of Samhain, the sea was grey again, and everything below was hidden from us. Late that day we sighted land ahead off our bow. Mael Duin ordered us to drop sails and row, but the shore was sandy and there were no currents. We could have sailed straight in. Farther up the beach there was a stand of young rowan trees. Most of these were past flower, and the branches were full of red-orange berries. Mael Duin told us the berries were poisonous.

There was no sign of sickness in his speech or looks. Away from Epona, and with the Viking dead, he was himself. He was strong. I didn't know if when we reached Erin he would stay on Loch Corrib or go to the Eoganacht, but I had no regrets for my actions.

That night, as we sat around the fire finishing our meal of crab and gannet, I wanted to speak to him about the navigation of the last part of our voyage, and I realized that he was not with us. I took a torch and walked up and down the beach looking for him, and then I went into the woods. There I found him naked, lying under the trees. I called him, but he didn't answer. He was staring at a faded white blossom beside his hand. I thought he was drunk. We had poteen from the curragh and I'd given Brian as much as he wanted, but I didn't see a flask anywhere in the trees. I called his name again, watching his chest, waiting for it to rise. I brought the torch closer. His face was cold. His lips were stained red. There was red-orange foam at the corner of his mouth. There were rowanberries all over the ground. I couldn't find a pulse in his neck at all. I got an arm under him, and his head dropped back. I screamed for the others.

We carried him out of the grove and put him down beside the fire. I ran down to the boat for a blanket to cover him, he was so cold. Brian was lying on the other side of the fire. When I passed him coming back, he asked, "Is he dead, Diuran?"

I said, "I don't know."

"He should have stayed with her."

"He had to see her as she really was. She would have killed him, just like she killed his father."

"He came with us out of honor. He did it for you."

"You don't know anything about it."

He turned back towards the fire. "No, I don't."

"He came with us because he's sane," I told him.

"Sane," he said, "but he just didn't want to live."

The night and day passed slowly. There was no life in him. At the end of the second day, they mourned him, and discussed what to do with his body. There were no rocks or caves on the island to build a cairn. Germane said we'd have to burn him. I said not yet. Mael Duin's body was cold, but his muscles were still tense. It seemed that the tension would leave him, not linger, if he were dead.

On the third morning the birds came. They circled and landed, coming closer and closer, getting so bold that I had to jump up and scream at them to keep them off. They screamed back, as if we were competing for the same prize. That day I took the thread out of Brian's wrist; it was healing well. When I came back around the fire and looked at Mael Duin, a breeze picked up a gold curl off his forehead and laid it down. I saw how pale he was, and then I knew that he was dead.

When a man has finished the seven years of ollam study, and can answer the high druid's questions and repeat all the old poetry without faltering, then he has one test remaining before he becomes a druid. He goes alone to a high place and he eats the poisonous rowan-berry. If in three days he has not died, or gone mad, he becomes a poet.

At the moment when I thought that Mael Duin was dead, he opened his eyes. Everyone cried with happiness. Someone brought him a piece of meat, but he would take water and nothing else. He wouldn't speak, but closed his eyes, and we left him alone to rest. Germane said, "He wants to hold on to his dreams." The poison was out of him when he awoke. He spoke very little about his dreams, only pieces now and then. He had seen a mountain breathe. At dusk the sun and clouds had reached down to a river and poured out fire. He saw green lamps inside every blade of grass on the riverbank. He saw the hearts inside birds of all kinds, even the vultures that circled his head, glowing through their feathers like brilliant rubies.

He asked us questions about the shapes of certain mountains, glens, and streams in Connemara and Wicklow. Some were places he had been himself, others he had never seen before. He'd listen to our descriptions intently, with his eyes closed, as though he might remember something important from his dreams. He seemed anxious to get home.

He wouldn't touch fish, birds or poteen. Music made him tense; he slept very little and ate only enough to stay alive. I never heard him speak Epona's name. But he spoke more gently to all of us, and while he had always been remote, now there was always someone with him, talking. His strength came back to him quickly. He pushed himself harder than before, and within three days we were following him to the other side of the island.

We walked through old woods of rowan and oak, then came out on the sea and followed the coast until it spread out in a flat plain. There was a small lake in it. A row of hills rose up from the far shore of the lake, and at the foot of the hills, beside it, there was a small stone church. An old man lived there and tended the sheep that ranged on the hills. He told us we were welcome to as much mutton as we could use.

We ate well that night, and the next morning we sent some men back with wool grease for the hull of our curragh. The sea was getting warmer, going south, and without the grease our hide boat would rot. It wasn't long after they left that Germane called out and pointed at the southwest sky. A huge bird dipped into the forest at the far end of the island and rose up heavily, carrying an enormous branch in its talons. It landed on the hill beside the lake, and lay on its side, exhausted, obviously old and weak. Still, we were afraid, and only Mael Duin would walk up to the edge of the hill to see what it would do. The bird ignored him. It hunched over the branch, and slowly began to eat the red berries among the leaves. The rest of us, armed with spears and shields, climbed the hill and joined Mael Duin.

While we stood watching, two eagles landed near the gigantic bird and began to groom him. They picked out the lice and old feathers and stripped away the scales of mange on his body. When they were finished they filled their beaks with berries and dropped them into the water. Then the huge bird went into the lake and washed himself. He stayed there until it had begun to grow dark. Then the eagles flew off and the bird came out of the water, his plumage clean and brilliant, and he flew with strong, broad strokes straight up into the sky.

Then I found myself running down the hill and into the lake. The cold water filled my mouth. I swam underwater and I could see the bottom of the lake clearly, a vast floor of smooth stones that seemed to go on forever.

When I came out of the lake I went to Mael Duin, and I saw the piece of silver mesh tied to his belt. I told him that I had done a terrible thing to him. A look of pain crossed his face, and I saw what I could do with the weight of my conscience, if I pressed him to forgive me. It was the virtue of the lake to prolong my life past the span of other men's, and know well how I could never repair what I'd done, or feel the cleansing curse of his anger.

The next day at sea we saw a falcon, and Mael Duin

ordered us to row in the direction that the bird had flown. Before nightfall, we came upon Inisheer, off the coast of Erin. We put into the island for the night, and went up together to a house above the rocks where there was light and noise.

A heavy man opened the door and let us in, then took us to a table and served us beer and Irish bread. At the table next to ours sat four or five men armed with Viking weapons. They were drinking and talking, not paying any attention to us at all. Mael Duin sat down with them.

In the years after our voyage, Germane met many Vikings, in battle and in trade, because he chose a life at sea. He never heard the name of Ailill Ocar Aga spoken. I stayed in Connemara, making boats. Mael Duin went east and built his monastery of Tamlacht in the mountains north of Wicklow, near the great cairns. There was little food and no music or poteen in his monastery, although visions were greatly respected. He called himself a Christian, and he cut himself off from women and pagans and the western sea.

Immram Curaig Mael Duin. The voyage of Mael Duin's boat is ended. Do not ask the meaning of it. I don't know where Mael Duin's power came from; from his madness, perhaps. I know nothing of waking dreams, or visions. It was a long time ago.

EPILOGUE

10

The boy was asleep beside the hearth. The last piece of turf was almost completely white. There was a stream of light coming in the cell window. Diuran smiled, turning the silver mesh over in his hand. In the early light it almost disappeared, as if it were nothing more substantial than the flecks of dust spiraling in the beam.

"You have completed the story," he said, folding his long, beautiful hands over the cloth. "Mael Duin left the monastery before the raid. He went back to her."

Breon stood up and walked away from the table. "That's impossible. Even if your obscene story is true, the man was ancient and frail. He never would have made it. It's a hard walk to the shore. And one long day in the sun at sea would have finished him."

"He could choose his death like any man," said the big man, rising and waking the boy. "One day or many days, it doesn't matter. It was his intention to return. Good night, then, or good day," he said, picking up his staff.

"Then I've been cheated." Breon stood in front of the door. "What was this man's magic? What have you told me? Something about a Viking sword—we already know that their weapons are superior. You've kept me up all night for something I already know. They're not the same person. I don't believe your story at all." He came back and looked Diuran in the face. "And you're no poet. You can't even tell a story well. There's no more sense to it than to drunken raving. You're a lunatic. And I'm old enough to be your grandfather myself." Then he reached for the piece of weaving in Diuran's hand. "I'll keep this. It belongs to the abbey, to the real Mael Duin of Tamlacht."

Diuran said, "No, you won't." He pushed the boy ahead of him, and they walked out the door.

Breon was shaking with anger. "Go on, Mael Muire, go after him. Watch which way he goes. Dear God, let him ride straight to the Vikings, he loves them so much. They'll show him how to steal from a monastery. We'll get the boys armed and the horses out. He's a madman— we could have been murdered—go on, hurry. . . ."

Mael Muire walked up the path to the stables. The snow had melted during the night, but the air was very cool; it was still early. There were small purple flowers all over the path. They were closed up, and the sun had not yet fallen on their petals. He passed the tower. A wren flew out of the high window.

At the top of the path, the boy was waiting. He nodded and Mael Muire passed him and went into the stable. It was warm and dark inside; the only light came from the door and from the rounded arched windows high above the stalls. This was a chapel once, he thought. Diuran came toward him, leading his horses. Mael Muire followed him out into the light.

Diuran put one hand on the horse's withers. He opened the other—there was the piece of silver fabric. "He left this for me. Maybe he could not come home. Maybe he belonged to her. I don't know. I never knew him."

Mael Muire walked with them up the hill to a place where the path went west and south. Diuran got up on his horse. He looked at the sky and ran his long fingers through his hair. "It's a fine day for a walk," he said. He held the yew staff out to Mael Muire.

Mael Muire watched them ride south until they disappeared in the birches. There was just a glimmer of sea beyond the crown of bright green leaves. He turned the druid's staff in his hand and found a good holding place. Then he took the path that led west over the mountain, where the new grass was coming up around the stones, and started home.